ABOUT THE AUTHOR

ANGELA SLATTER is a Brisbane-based writer of speculative fiction. She has a Masters (Research) in Creative Writing, which produced *Black-Winged Angels*, a short story collection of reloaded fairytales, and is undertaking a PhD in Creative Writing. During her daylight hours, she works at a writers' centre.

Her short stories have appeared in anthologies such as Jack Dann's *Dreaming Again*, Tartarus Press' *Strange Tales II* and *III*, Ann and Jeff VaderMeer's *Steampunk Reloaded*, Twelfth Planet Press' *2012*, Dirk Flinthart's *Canterbury 2100*, and in journals such as *Lady Churchill's Rosebud Wristlet*, *Shimmer*, ONSPEC and *Doorways Magazine*. Her work has had several Honourable Mentions in the Datlow, Link, Grant *Year's Best Fantasy and Horror* anthologies #20 and #21; and three of her stories have been shortlisted for the Aurealis Awards in the Best Fantasy Short Story category.

She is working on a duopoly, *Well of Souls* and *Gate of the Dead*, and alternative Crusades saga, as well as *Finbar's Mother*, a Norse-Irish fantasy. She is a graduate of Clarion South 2009 and the Tin House Summer Writers Workshop 2006. In 2010, she will have two short story collections published, *Sourdough & Other Stories* with Tartarus Press (UK) and *The Girl with No Hands & Other Tales* (Ticonderoga Publications). This makes her happy.

ABOUT THE ARTIST

LISA HANNETT lives in Adelaide, South Australia—city of churches, bizarre murders, and pie floaters. She has sold stories to venues including *Clarkesworld* Magazine, *Fantasy* Magazine, *Weird Tales*, *Electric Velocipede*, *ChiZine*, and the *Steampunk Reloaded* anthology. Her story "On the Lot and In the Air" appeared on the *Locus* Recommended Reading List for 2009. Lisa is a graduate of the Clarion South Writers Workshop. When she's not writing, she does graphic design work and chips away at her never-ending PhD thesis.

THE GIRL WITH NO HANDS
AND OTHER TALES

ALSO BY ANGELA SLATTER

Sourdough & Other Stories (collection)
(Tartarus Press, 2010)

THE GIRL WITH
NO HANDS
AND OTHER TALES

ANGELA
SLATTER

TICONDEROGA
PUBLICATIONS

Dedicated to my family, for all their patience and care

PATRONS

The Author and Publisher wish to thank the following for their support of independent press and valued contribution to this title's publication.

Kate Eltham
Meg Vann
Jodi de Vantier
Kirstyn McDermott
Daniel Simpson
Michelle Slatter

ACKNOWLEDGEMENTS

Thanks to all the people who helped me get these stories published in the first place, with particular thanks to: the Shimmery crew (Beth Wodzinski, Lisa Mantchev, Joy Marchand, E. Catherine Tobler, Mary Robinette Kowal); Gavin Grant and Kelly Link of Lady Churchill's Rosebud Wristlet; *the inimitable Jack Dann; Ronnie Scott and* The Lifted Brow *Gang; Jeff and Ann VanderMeer; Cat Rambo and Sean Wallace and Molly Tanzer at* Fantasy Magazine.

And a huge extra special thanks to Lisa Hannett for the cover and the beta-reading and the perspicacious comments; and also to Russell at Ticonderoga, without whom this collection would not have been possible.

CONTENTS

Caressing with Razors, by Jack Dann 13

Bluebeard 23

The Living Book 35

The Jacaranda Wife 43

Red Skein 55

The Chrysanthemum Bride 65

Frozen 77

The Hummingbird Heart 85

Words 93

The Little Match Girl 101

The Juniper Tree 107

Skin 119

The Bone Mother 125

The Dead Ones Don't Hurt You 139

Light As Mist, Heavy As Hope 151

Dresses, Three 167

The Girl With No Hands 179

Afterword, by Angela Slatter 197

CARESSING WITH RAZORS

JACK DANN

So (you may ask) what the hell is all this fuss over Angela Slatter?

Well, this introduction probably isn't going to help you very much with that ... I can sing and dance, jump up and down, shill in my shrill, crowded room voice about how wonderful these stories are; but you, oh, inquisitive and perspicacious readers, will swiftly make up your own minds when you read the wry, poignant, and eviscerating stories that follow. All *I* can hope to do is give you a few facts and my own take on the work of this fabulously talented writer.

You've probably already guessed the nefarious and sinister purpose of this introduction: that it's actually an advertisement, a marketing ploy/exercise to put you in the proper frame of mind to read this short story collection 'correctly' and create what we used to call 'the halo effect' in the madmen marketing business. The hopes and prayers of ad-men (and ad-women!) are that what you first see, hear, read, sense, and experience will positively affect how you feel about what comes later.

I don't deny my job here is that of author's shill ... and, of course, you can guess (yet again) what comes next: a vigorous assertion that Angela Slatter's wicked stories don't need any pumping by me or anyone else; but Angela isn't famous *yet*, although I will bet you a dollar and a shot of the best unblended whisky at the bar that she will become a major literary voice. I'll tell you why I think that, but it's really not necessary to read me prattling on: just page forward to stories such as "The Jacaranda Wife" or "The Chrysanthemum Bride" or "The Little Match Girl" or "The Bone Mother" or the title story "The Girl with No Hands"; and *then* when your mind is stretched, blown, and (temporarily) broken, you'll know why literary and genre insiders are so excited about this writer.

However, if you're not from the school of what we Pleistocenes' used to call New Criticism, then perhaps a very few words about Ms Slatter and her work might shed some light on the 'after-experience' of reading her stories.

Angela Slatter is a young, beautiful, gregarious, extremely bright and funny no-nonsense writer who is polite and generous, but who I imagine would not suffer fools gladly. Her writing, which seems transparent as glass, as if so easily and simply wrought, belies the complete control of craft and the complexity of the material floating and glinting and shifting just under the surface. Her concerns are the primordial fears of childhood ... and adulthood: the dark, slimy, senescent fairytale monsters that threaten to chop off our fingers when we suck our thumbs, burn us to death if we play with matches, or turn us into pale, thin, little corpses if we won't eat our soup ... the same monsters— albeit transmogrified into suits and skirts—that stalk us even now and threaten to maim us yet again as we flee that dangerous, ill-remembered country called childhood. Slatter has said, "My writing is an act of absolute fear ... Perhaps that is why I write of fearful things: first fears, primal fears. Fear of the dark, of things we do not know, of being abandoned, of not being loved, of not being smart/beautiful/brave enough: fear of not knowing the rules."

This is the dark heart of all serious fiction, whether it be literary or genre; but the stories that are fueled by the freshest, most oxygenated blood, the stories that reflect and refract our fears in their purest, most fundamental and personal form, are ... fairytales. The seemingly simple, didactic and innocent fairytale is one of the most potent and direct expressions of our unconscious ... and it is also the heart, blood, and nerves of the disquietly powerful, transformative stories in this collection.

But Slatter the scholar, academic, and feminist understands that that when fairytales were translated from oral to written form by Charles Perrault, Hans Christian Anderson, and the Brothers Grimm, these writers subtly changed many of the tales told to them by young and old women ... transformed them to suit their own male agendas and social and religious aesthetics. They in effect 'colonised' the tales, which then became parental and societal tools to socialise and control children ... and teach them their 'proper' gender roles. Slatter has said:

"Colonised fairytales offer us, women and men, a particular mode of living and interacting. If you do not fit this mould, then you are doomed; you can only be an ugly stepsister or a wicked stepmother, or one of the princesses who do not win the prince because you do not follow the rules. What do I do with fairytales? When I rewrite them I try to offer a different view, a different mode of being, a path of shared equality, not merely a simple inversion ...

"When I write, when I rewrite my fears, I'm sending them back out into the world refracted. I hold them up to a light and turn things ever so slightly—I suppose I learned at one point that it is all about how *you* look at things in life."

Although her stories deftly explode the patriarchal messages embedded in traditional fairytales, Slatter bears the burden of being a *real* writer: her stories are organic; they live and breathe on their own and for themselves; they transform their didactic elements into mortal flesh and fire; they teach us uneasy truths. And they remind us that *we* are the wicked stepmothers and ugly stepsisters.

We are the doomed stepfathers and ugly brothers.

We are the ones who can't—or won't—follow the rules.

Although I had expected to go on (and on, God help us) from here and tell you fresh, tantalising, and amusing anecdotes about the author, I can't help but notice that this introduction just ended (as if by its own will and intention) with the paragraph above.

I should mention at this point that we writers *really* are in complete control of our material (rather than the material 'knowing' how to find its own destination at its own pace and time or, heaven forefend, being in control of the author), but perhaps my dark, nasty and ill-spoken unconscious is telling me to shut the hell up and let you get on to read the stories. So ... make sure you have enough light lest you strain your eyes. You'll probably also need a strong night-light in the bedroom tonight. Just to protect you from the scaly, razor-fanged, salivating, famished, scissor-handed zombie creatures that will soon be escaping from the oily depths of your reawakened and revitalised id.

Angela's stories seem to have that affect on people.

Sweet dreams, gentle readers ...

Jack Dann
Windhover Farm
Victoria, Australia
July 2010

THE OTHER TALES

BLUEBEARD

BLUEBEARD

Her breath smells like champagne, but not bitter as you might expect.

Something inside her turns it sweet, I'm not sure what. She's a sugar-candy kind of girl, bright and crystalline as she reclines on the sofa—a *chaise longue*, more correctly. Her hair is spun like golden sugar, her eyebrows so light they may as well not be there, her lashes so contrastingly black that they must be dyed, her skin pale pink, and her mouth a rosebud pout, filled with small pearly teeth. Around her neck curls a long string of beads, wrapped twice and still long enough to hang to her waist. The dress is diaphanous, shimmering yellow, damp in places with traces of her last client. She is nothing if not *lush*. She catches me looking and smiles.

"How's my girl doing?" Her voice is honey, smooth, practiced, as though I'm one of her 'patrons'.

I sit primly on the edge of my seat, hands clasped in my lap, knees together, shiny black shoes snug against one another, my pink dress stretched as far over my knees as it will go.

"I'm fine, Mother." I study the pile of books on the corner table. "Did Davide leave those for me?"

"Yes, Lily. More books for my little genius, my little pearl," she says, still smiling but crookedly now; my mother doesn't like my intellect.

One of her regulars, Davide, the banker, leaves us both gifts: for her it's money, gems and a stickiness between her thighs; for me, it's books. He thinks it funny that his whore's child is smart, a grownup brain in a ten-year-old body. He is a large man, a *nouvours*, a teddy bear. Davide pays for my schooling, too, an expensive convent school where the nuns pretend they don't know what my mother does.

Mother thinks it's unnecessary: schooling, reading, thinking. She's not dumb herself, but believes the only brains a girl needs are the soft, wet pink ones between her legs. Better pink matter than grey matter. And she's done well for herself: she owns an apartment in Paris (such a long way from her early life in America's South), and she's got money in the bank, so we don't live hand-to-mouth like so many whores and their children.

We did for a time. When we first came here, we lived in a brothel hung heavily with red velvet draperies, and run by a Madam whose over-abundant flesh struggled with the confines of her gown. At first, I made friends with the children of other whores, but they were ephemeral creatures and after the third one disappeared I stopped bothering. Soon enough, Mother prospered and we left.

She hasn't tried to sell me to some man with a taste for young flesh. Some women sell their daughters' virginity for a fortune; the worst of them have the girls sewn up and sold again and again until some man gets wise to the scar tissue. The very, very worst sell their children's lives altogether, but few people speak of that. It only happens in dark places, places where the air is heavy and sounds are strangely muffled as though crossing a great space, places where what's normal ceases to have any influence. Places we will not go.

Of course, Mother doesn't refer to herself as a *whore*—it's what I do in my thoughts. She calls herself a *courtesan* but it's all the same, really. Money for cunt, whichever way you slice it.

My mother looks like a pearl in a baroque setting. I try to analyse her—have done so my whole short life—as if she's some rock that I can break down to its elements. I try to write her history, too, in my mind, as if it will help me make sense of her, as if I can trace the patterns and paths of her life and she will suddenly become comprehensible to me. As if my clever little brain will finally crack the one puzzle I can't seem to work out.

"Davide's asked us to go away for the weekend," she says casually.

I raise an eyebrow, an expression cynical in an adult, impertinent in a child; another parent would slap me for it. "You mean he's invited *you*, Mother."

"No, both of us. He's got this big house just outside the Bois de Boulogne. It's not so far, honey. His mama stays there most of the time but she's away visiting her sister. Davide wants us to keep him company for the weekend. Maybe longer."

"What about school?"

"Hell, Davide pays their ridiculous fees. Those old penguins will just have to shut up and bear it." My mother has issues with nuns, not surprisingly. "The car will come for us on Friday afternoon."

"What about his mother? What will she say if she finds out?" I ask, probing, knowing she'll hate it.

"We don't need to know that, do we? We don't need to ask questions." Her teeth are gritted, her smile tight. I'll let her go now, release her from the hook of my curiosity.

So we're off to the countryside.

I'm a child of cities, of cobbled streets, of tall houses that block out the sun. I'm a child who knows how to weave among the legs of a crowd like a nimble rat. How will I know what to do in treed spaces where no noise rushes by one's ears in a hurry to go wherever noise goes?

It's dark when we arrive.

The house is big and old. It sits in its park, dark and pock-marked, ivy growing across it like moss on the back of a toad that's been sitting too long in one place. I can see, through one of the windows, a tiny light inside, coming closer as its bearer glides forward.

Davide opens the door for my mother, and the driver opens mine. I struggle out, pushing against the darkness that swarms outside the safety of the automobile. It's like a dog, too big, too friendly and I run to press myself against my mother's legs, for once acting my age, thinking that all the protection I need is there. Her hands stroke my hair, curl around my earlobes and hold me briefly, then she takes the arm Davide offers, catches at my suddenly cold hand and we move toward the opening door of the house.

The man there is old, straight in the manner of those who pride themselves on not succumbing to the rigours of age, handsome in a silvered way, snide in his look at my mother and I. There's that quick flash of disapproval—his kind sometimes recognize my mother's in a moment, servants and whores being close kin. Perhaps the servant recognizes this kinship and so despises anyone who reminds him of it.

Any road, it's obvious. He will cover his disdain for my mother, at least while his master is around; he will not bother with me, for I am a child, and a whore's child at that. Who will care if I complain?

We are led to a dining room and a sumptuous table set with more food than three people have any hope of getting through. Perhaps there are more servants in this house and they will benefit, or maybe it will go to the church and the priest will give it to his flock. Or the priest and his fat housekeeper will gorge themselves silly before they go off to bed and sin against their god, the priest burying his busy prick between her rosy thighs like a spade in damp soil.

I was born a cynic.

Above the fireplace hangs a portrait. The woman is large-boned, with a heavy jaw and thick lips. Her hair is pulled back severely, defying the frivolity of her silver-pink ball dress. She holds a Chinese fan in masculine hands, seemingly caught in the moment just before she breaks it in a cold rage. I don't think I would like her.

"That's my mother, little one." Davide has caught the direction of my gaze. "It was painted during her season in Paris, before she married my father."

I nod dutifully and turn my attention back to the plate in front of me.

My mother and Davide talk and I drowse over my meal. I slip sideways in the high, over-stuffed chair and press my head against my mother's breasts. Her hand is tender if a little distracted, then Davide hoists me like a doll; he is a big man, a bear who's been shaved and taught to walk upright. His smile is strange and his eyes are yellow. He smells like ambergris.

He tucks me into a large bed on the second floor. My mother has stripped away my navy school uniform but has neglected to slip the white nightgown over my head. She turns away and folds the uniform as her lover pulls the thick linen sheet up to cover me. His huge hands skim my flat chest; I cannot tell if it's deliberate or not. He rubs a palm over my cheeks then dips his thick thumb in my mouth quickly, before my mother turns around.

I am a child. I am tired. I am afraid and removed from all the anchors of my normal life. My mother would not believe me. Something in his face tells me there's no intent there, merely a kind of cruel curiosity to see if whore's blood runs through my veins too. He has shown no interest in me before. Perhaps I passed his test; I did not react.

My mother's lips are soft on my forehead as she whispers goodnight. Davide is at the door before she pulls back and stands to survey me a moment, smiling. My mother loves me, this I know, but I do not know if she loves me best.

Keys. So many keys.

I'm sitting at a battered table in the kitchen. An old woman, who could do with a wash, smiles as I eat the porridge she prepared for me.

I don't like porridge but I'm a polite child when it comes to food. I spoon the gruel into my mouth and distract myself by counting the keys hanging on a myriad of hooks on the kitchen wall. If I'm good, I hope she'll let me have some of the fresh bread she's just pulled from the oven. I will have it smothered with the yellowest of butters and the reddest of the jams that sit on the far end of the table. I can almost convince myself that the porridge is worth it.

My mother and Davide have not yet risen. Or perhaps they have risen and gone out for the day. Perhaps there are stables and they have gone riding. Does my mother know how to ride something other than a man?

The keys catch my attention again. Some are very old, dark, others new, brassy and shiny. This is therefore a house of many doors—otherwise, why all these keys? Maybe there are rooms no one goes into anymore and the keys languish here, forgotten and unused. There is one empty hook and I wonder on it. Is the room locked, a sealed space, its key lost? Or is the key kept elsewhere, hidden, and the room a sacred place guarded from casual intrusion?

I finish my porridge and cook lets me have some bread and jam. I eat until I feel sick—bitter in the knowledge that if I hadn't eaten the porridge I would have been able to eat more bread. Next time, I'll refuse the gruel.

Cook shoos me out of the kitchen. As I pass the keys my eyes slip over the empty space, my fingers twitching as if curling around a key that is not there.

The library is huge.

I love the smell, the perfume of ink and paper. A book sits in my lap; it is small but so am I. I curl in the corner of an old armchair and carefully turn the pages. The lives of saints glow under my tiny fingers, their faces beatific despite the torments their bodies are suffering, caught eternally in pain on the paper. All the saints here are women.

I found the tome on the desk in front of the arched window. It looks well-thumbed, the pages falling open as willingly as a whore's legs. It has an embroidered cover, fine white linen with religious icons running rampant across it, crucifixes, praying hands, angels' wings. I wonder if it's Davide's mother who fondles this book, her hands touching the faces, envying them their beauty, their pain, their martyrdom. My mother would not understand. She is beautiful but she is no martyr. Nor a saint.

It is late and I wonder where she is. I have not seen her or Davide all day. The butler would not answer me when I asked him at lunch. The cook gave me pitying looks. I retreated to the library. My mother will know to find me here.

I must have fallen asleep.

I am still nestled in the armchair but the book has fallen from my lap. Its spine has split and the pages are askew. I want to hide it but I know its owner will come looking.

I bend and collect the pages. Under the leaves of parchment lies a key, quite small, heart-shaped at the end, black with age. I think perhaps it lived in the spine of the book but now I have destroyed its home. I slip it into the pocket of my pinafore and finish gathering the scattered folios.

It's dark outside once again.

I make my way to the dining room, damaged book in hand. Davide sits alone at the laden table. I approach and settle the book next to him.

"I'm sorry, Davide. I dropped it and the spine—it broke," I say in a small voice. His great head turns and yellow eyes look at me as if they have to try hard to focus. There's a scratch on his neck, just above the collar of his shirt and a smear of blood on his ear as if he's washed carelessly. I don't step back.

"Things break, little one. It can be fixed. Books can be fixed." He picks the thing up and turns it over; his hand moves across the cover the same way they have moved across my mother's skin.

"Where's my mother?"

His eyes focus on me at last, sharp. "Sleeping, Lily. She's very tired."

"Oh."

He reaches out and twines his fingers in my hair, like my mother does. "You're not afraid, are you? What a strange child you are."

I don't answer him and he continues.

"Would you like to stay here? You and your mother?"

"I'm sure *your* mother would not be happy with us as houseguests, Davide."

"Mother won't know, little pearl." He echoes my mother's name for me. "But this could be the perfect place for you both. You would be lovely additions to my collection."

I try to step back but he still holds my curls in his great paw. I cannot pull away without losing a hank of hair. His eyes darken and I think I see the bear inside, not so deep now, but near the surface—he is no longer *nouvours* but something dangerous, something that looks kind but will swat me aside without thinking, something that will shred me like a kitten between a dog's teeth. He leans toward me, his breath rank as raw meat.

"How will you grow, little pearl? Will you be like her?" The fingers of his other hand catch at the hem of my skirt, flicking it up as scornfully as a breeze, but they go no further. "Will you be like her? A whore? Shall I wait for you to grow, little pearl? Will you replace your mother for me?"

I pull away, heedless of the pain, and he lets me go, laughing.

I do not know this man. This man who beds my mother. This man who pays for my schooling. This man who brings me books to read. This man who scares me half to death. This man who pushes back his chair and begins to rise.

I run.

The door is black. The bars of iron across it are rusted in places.

The pattern on its lock echoes the heart shape of the key sitting heavily in my pocket. I put my eye to the keyhole.

The light is dim inside and I cannot make out much. There is white, there is red, there is black. If I cannot find my mother, I will hide here until daylight.

To my surprise the key turns easily. The lock is well-oiled, often-used. Someone comes here a lot. Perhaps it is Davide's mother. I push the door hard.

Things hang on the walls and lie on the floor at the edges of the room. Bones scattered like pearls in the dim light of the brazier. At the end of the room is a bed, a four-poster draped with sheer curtains. Something lies white and glimmering there. I tiptoe through the bones as if they are daisies in the garden of my convent school. I must not disturb them or the nuns will be angry.

The drapes stick to my hand as if the fabric has sweated in the heat of the room. My mother lies on the soiled coverlet. She is white with red stripes across her skin. One side of her face is swollen and her lips are the purple-black of dried blood.

I think she is dead. I reach out and struggle with the cords that bind her wrists to the bed. Then those at her ankles. It's not right that she be like this: splayed and displayed without her consent, without her will. She wouldn't want to look like one of those saints; there is no beauty in her pain. Whoever imagined the saints took their pleasure thus surely had not seen them like this.

My hand hovers over her face. I want to touch her skin, to know if it's warm or cold, to see if there is breath left in her, but I am pulled away.

"Little whore." The voice is old, brittle as a cinder, and breathes the words as if they bring joy. I struggle, my hair blinding me. I am thrown across the room and land in a pile of bones. A rib pierces my side and I cry out.

"Whore's daughter," comes the voice again and I brush the hair out of my eyes.

A woman looks down at me, eager as a hunting dog.

Her dress was once fine, black silk crepe with severe pintucks stitched by slavish fingers, but now it's dusty and dirty, encrusted with something that may once have been liquid but now makes the fabric as stiff as a corpse. At her breast hangs a heavy wooden penitent's cross, plain, the figure of Christ rubbed featureless by devout caresses. She leers down at me.

"Too curious, little whore, just like that one." Her voice drops to a whisper. "My son tries to keep them from me, but they always find their way here, they all come to be cleansed. Does your blood run as quickly as theirs, I wonder?"

Hers is the face from the dining room portrait, with its disapproving glare. Her hands are the ones that lovingly caressed the book of saints, longingly consuming their agony. She comes for me with surprising speed.

My hand closes on the broken rib that drips with my blood. As she leans down, hands reaching for me, I jam it into her eye.

She screams, jerks, then I hear a wet thud as a second blow falls and she slumps forward. I scramble out of the way of her falling bulk. Another bone protrudes from her back.

My mother stands behind her and she is the most beautiful thing I have ever seen.

A shadow falls across the doorway and Davide enters, his step hesitant. He seems unwilling to meet my mother's eyes. When he does, he whimpers. I watch her face and she is terrible as an army with banners. She is naked and bloodied, yet there is something about her that will not be quenched. He did not save her from this danger and he will not be forgiven.

When Davide sees *his* mother, his cry is painfully loud. Mother and I limp from the room, leaving him to gather up her body, a reversed pieta.

The door closes slowly behind us and my mother, with only a moment's hesitation, turns the heart-shaped key in the lock.

THE LIVING BOOK

THE LIVING BOOK

"Sophia," says my father, "I need something to read. Come here."

I present myself dutifully, and he peels back my shirt so as to expose the shifting, changing lines of printed word.

Here I stand: Sophia, the Living Book.

I was born in Byzantium. Or made. Yes, rather made. And father is not Father, but Maker, a bookbinder of extraordinary talent. He made me for the Emperor Constantine, who loved me for many years, in many ways, until his religion got the better of him.

Perhaps he read inappropriate words in my face when he made love to me, or on my back when he took me that way. Inescapable words that made him think what he did was sinful rather than joyous. I find it hard, still, to hide what I am thinking; some days I have to concentrate on some innocuous tale or I'll be in ever so much trouble.

I lived in the palace with all the other treasures Constantine collected. My rooms were sumptuous, glorious spaces hung with silks and gold. I had servants to do my whim—mutes, who could not read, and so could tell no one of what they saw or whom they served. I was a strange princess, Constantine's greatest, most beloved secret.

One day, though, he decided his precious things should be displayed, that his people and visitors should be impressed and awed by his wealth, so he might prove himself the greatest of rulers through sheer weight of possessions. Thus the Parade of Great Treasures was born, short-lived abortion of a thing it was.

They placed me in the lead chariot so I might be first among the treasures, and naked so that the Emperor's subjects would see all the glory of the written word. I had never been out among people, I was overwhelmed, words tore across my skin like mad ants, so that I seemed blackened by the crawling serifs. The crowds lining the streets panicked, rioted with fear, stampeded. Thousands were killed. It's one of those events that was written out of history—but it lives on in me. If I think of it, or Father asks for it, the tale appears on me, on the leaves of my flesh, never forgotten. History I keep pristine; but with the *fabula* I play.

When calm was finally restored and the dead had been buried, Constantine retired with his pet priest, the Patriarch, to contemplate how his pride had brought about the disaster. I, being female, not quite human, a receptacle of truth and lies, was no favourite of the dried up old priest. He had been in the emperor's ear for years, trying to convince him that I was intrinsically wicked. He finally succeeded, his pleas lent weight by the piles of corpses Constantine had inadvertently caused.

He couldn't destroy me, Constantine, because I was too wondrous, too strange, too much loved. For a while he gave me to his concubine but she tired of me soon enough—her liking was for traditional tales, stories that were static, their endings known and predictable. I changed my stories just to annoy her.

Finally, though, it was exile. Moved from tower to tower, castle to castle, from Nicosia to Alexandria, from Paris to Prague, shuffled and shifted like a volume on a shelf and always in the care of Father. What his extended span cost him in other people's lives I have often wondered. I wonder, too, what I am to him. Am I just a thing he made, evidence of his genius? Would he, like the great sculptor, Praxitiles, simply put his mark on me? Am I merely something to bear the words *Libanius made me*?

Does he love me at all? Am I a source of pride but not affection? These are the things that prick at me. He does not answer these questions—never has, so I stopped asking after the first hundred years. But these thoughts fester. I'm not an ordinary book; I record what I see, learn, experience and process. I *feel*.

We've been in New York for almost one hundred years, in this strangest of all strange places. A bizarre and overwhelming mix of too many influences and cultures and people living on top of each other. I used to go out at night but it's too dangerous now, and in today's world I cannot afford to be found.

In the early years I could go to the dim, dark clubs; no one really noticed me or if they did, they simply thought me tattooed. I liked *Elaine's*—at its height, I loved to go there and mingle with the great writers of the day. I wanted to say *Here I am, word made flesh!* But I didn't, of course, I didn't; that would have angered Father and his punishments are worse than anything. Centuries ago I realised that he wouldn't burn me no matter how many times he threatened it; what sacrilege to destroy such a wonder! But he knows other ways to hurt and harm, so I am wary of aggravating him.

I told one man though; I liked Hemingway, big burly man with his booming voice, his beautiful written words, and his tiny prick. I knew his secret and he knew mine. I was a fascination to him, a place for him to worship even though the rest of his life was godless. When Father found I'd spoken the truth of what I was, he locked me in the library (how apt a prison!). He flew to Spain; and then Hemingway was gone.

This latest tower is a venerable penthouse, in a neighbourhood of money so old it creaks. Neighbours politely ignore each other, believing that other people's business is precisely that. Sometimes they speak though—I hear them when sound travels up the elevator shafts, and the ventilation shafts, or when I press my ear tightly to the wall—of the handsome old man, and his daughter kept inside by her rare skin condition.

The rooms are large, airy. Mine I keep much as it was in Byzantium. Oh, very few of the fittings are original, time has turned those to dust, but I recreate my first world as well as I can. There are wall hangings and draperies that I love, and the jewellery given to me by the Emperor lives in velvet-lined caskets. I made Father find me proper Turkish carpets for my floors. Two walls are lined with books. For some years I would sit very close to them, thinking they would tell me their secrets in a voice only I could hear; but no, they are dumb siblings, giving up their stories only when their covers are cracked open, and eyes and brain practise their peculiar exchange with the paper.

I love our living room best of all, with its huge bank of glass windows, so the sky seems endless. It looks like freedom, all that sky. Sometimes I think about jumping; running hard at the glass and feeling it break under my weight, and falling, falling, with the wind blowing through me. Would I lose all form, become pages that scatter to the four winds or would I simply *splat* on the pavement?

I don't think I will try that. I have found my capacity for learning is infinite—or at least, I haven't yet found any limits. I pull in new information, learn how to apply it, convert it to knowledge so nothing goes to waste. At first it was just from my fellows, books; then came the computers, and from them I have learned *much*. I especially like the idea of data transfer and there is a theory I have been moving about in my head for some time.

So, as I stand before Father, before *Maker*, as he flips through the story on my body, I stare out the window and think on his myriad cruelties. The grey winter sky seems like the expanse of his heart, a bleak and empty space. I think how I've only ever been a curious toy to him, a matter of perverse pride; never a daughter, only a *thing*.

I place my hands over his temples and smile, leaning in to kiss him on the lips. I feel the grey of his moustache tickle and the soft dryness of his lips. And I begin to draw, to download from him, everything he knows. I suck from him everything he is, ever has been, everything he ever knew. I read him like a stone carved with Linear B, and lick down the words. I continue until I've taken all juice, all moisture, all stories from him. His struggles lessen, cease, and a greying husk of a man slumps in the chair. I'll feed him to the fire soon, he's as dry and dusty as parchment; the flames will love him.

I scan everything that was him, now nesting in me, and find nothing that could be love: just that wicked pride.

I think, courtesy of my cousin the PC, that I may have solved the problem of my skin showing my story: wallpaper. I shall think myself blank, and as I walk through this world no one will be able to judge this book by her cover.

THE JACARANDA WIFE

THE JACARANDA WIFE

Sometimes, not very often, but sometimes when the winds blow right, the summer heat is kind, and the rain trickles down just-so, a woman is born of a jacaranda tree.

The indigenous inhabitants leave these women well alone. They know them to be foreign to the land for all that they spring from the great tree deeply embedded in the soil. White-skinned as the moon, violet-eyed, they bring only grief.

So when, in 1849, James Willoughby found one such woman sleeping beneath the spreading boughs of the old jacaranda tree in his house yard, members of the Birbai tribe who had once quite happily come to visit the kitchens of the station, disappeared. As they went, they told everyone they encountered, both black and white, that one of the pale women had come to Rollands Plain station and there would be no good of her. Best to avoid the place for a long, long time.

Willoughby, the younger son of an old Sussex family, had fought with his father, migrated to Australia, and made his fortune, in that order. His property stretched across ten thousand acres, and the Merino sheep he'd purchased from John McArthur thrived on the green, rolling pastures spotted with eucalypts and jacarandas. He had a house built from buttery sandstone, on a slight rise, surrounded on three sides by trees and manicured lawns, a turning circle out the front for carriages. Willoughby made sure the windows were wide enough to drink in the bright Australian light, and filled its rooms with all the finest things that reminded him of England. His one lack was that of a wife.

He had in his possession, it must be said, a large collection of miniatures sent by the parents of potential brides. Some were great beauties—and great beauties did not wish to live in the Colonies. Some were obviously plain, in spite of efforts the portraitists had gone to imbue them with some kind of charm; these girls were quite happy to make the arduous journey to a rich, handsome, dark-haired husband, but *he* did not want a plain wife. He had not made his way in the world to ornament this place with a plain-faced woman, no matter how sweet her nature might be.

The silver-haired girl he found early one morning was beyond even his dreams and demands. Long-limbed, delicate, with skin so pale he could see blue veins pulsing beneath her skin—for she was naked, sleeping on a bed of brilliant purple jacaranda flowers, crushed by the weight and warmth of her body. As he leaned over her, she opened her eyes and he was lost in their violet depths.

Ever the gentleman, he wrapped his proper Englishman's coat about her shoulders, speaking to her in the low, gentle voice he reserved for skittish horses, and steered her inside. He settled her on his very own bed, the place he had always hoped to bring a suitable wife, and called for his housekeeper. The broad, red-faced Mrs Flynn bustled in. She was a widow, living now with Willoughby's overseer in a fine arrangement that suited both of them. In Ireland, her three sons had been hung for treason against the British, and the judge who sentenced them decided that a woman who had produced three such anarchists must herself have strong anti-English sympathies. She was arrested, charged, tried and sent to live in this strange land with an arid centre and a wet green edge. She'd been allocated to Willoughby, and although her heart would always have a hole in it where her sons had been torn away, she had, in some measure, come to feel maternal about her master and directed her energies to making him happy as only a mother could.

The sight of the girl on the bed, lids shut once again, and the mooncalf look in her master's eyes troubled her but she held her tongue, pushed her greying red hair back under its white cap and began to bustle around the girl. Willoughby sat and stared.

"She's perfect, Martha. Don't you think?"

"Beautiful for sure, Master James, for all she's underdressed. Who is she? Where's she from?" Mrs Flynn surreptitiously sniffed at the girl's mouth for a whiff of gin. Finding nothing, her suspicions shifted; surely the girl was addle-pated. Or a tart, left adrift by a client of the worst sort. Or a convict on the run. Or a good girl who'd had something unspeakable visited upon her. She'd check later, to see if there was any bleeding. "Perhaps the doctor …"

"Is she hurt?" The urgency in his voice pierced her heart and she winced, like a good mother.

"Not that I can see, but we'd best be sure. Send for Dr Abrams. Go on now." She urged him from the room, her hands creating a small breeze as she flapped at him. Turning back to the girl, she found the violet eyes open once more, staring around her, without fear, and with only a mild curiosity.

"And what's your name, little miss?" Mrs Flynn asked, adjusting the blanket she'd laid over the girl. The eyes widened, the mouth opened but the only thing that came out was a noise like the breeze rushing through leaves.

Martha Flynn felt cold all over. Her bladder threatened to betray her and she had to rush from the room and relieve herself outside. She wore her sweat like a coat when she returned (it had taken all of her courage to step back inside). The girl eyed her mildly, a little sadly perhaps, but something in her gaze told Martha Flynn that she had been *entrusted* with a secret. It moved her fear to pity.

"Now then, the doctor will be here soon. You make yourself comfortable, *mavourneen*."

"She's a mute, you see," explained Willoughby to the parson. "No family that we can find. Someone has to look after her."

The Reverend St John Clare cleared his throat, playing for time before he had to answer. Willoughby saved him for a moment.

"She seems fond enough of me," he lied a little. She *seemed* not to hate him, nor anyone else. Even 'fond' was too strong a term, but he didn't want to say "She seems slightly less than indifferent to me." Sometimes she smiled, but mostly when she was outdoors, near the tree he'd found her under. She was neither grateful for his rescue, nor ungrateful; she simply took whatever was offered, be it protection, affection, or food (she preferred vegetables to meat, screwing her nose up at the plates of lamb and mutton). She did, however, take some joy in the new lambs, helping Mrs Flynn to care for them, feeding the motherless ones by hand, and they would follow her.

He'd named her Emily, after his grandmother. She had taken up painting; Willoughby had presented her with a set of watercolours, thinking it would be a lady-like way for her to pass the time. She sat outside and painted the jacaranda tree over and over, her skill growing with each painting, until she had at last produced a finely detailed, subtly rendered image, which Willoughby had framed. It hung over the fireplace in his study; he would stare it for hours, knowing there was something he was missing, some construction of line and curve, some intersection of colour he had failed to properly see. She would smile whenever she found him thus engaged, lightly drop her hand to his shoulder and finally leave as quietly as she had come.

"Does she want to marry you?" asked the parson.

"I think so. It's ..." struggled Willoughby, "it's just so damned inappropriate to have her under my roof like this! She's not a relative, she's not a ward, she's a woman and I ..."

"You love her," finished St John. Mrs Flynn had spoken to him quietly upon his arrival. "There's always a charitable institution? I could find her a position with one of the ladies in Sydney Town, as a maid or companion?"

"No! I won't let her go!" Willoughby wiped the sweat from his brow, felt his shirt sticking to the skin of his back. "I can't let her go. I want to look after her. I want her to wife."

St John Clare released a heavy sigh. He was, to a large extent, dependent on Willoughby's good will—what mind did it make to him if Willoughby wished to marry a mute who'd appeared from nowhere? Younger sons were still kidnapping brides in England—this was marginally less reprehensible. "Very well. I will conduct the ceremony. Next Sunday?"

"Tomorrow."

"Ah, yes, tomorrow. Very well." He did not use the phrase 'unseemly haste', although he knew others would. What Willoughby wanted, Willoughby would have, and if it benefited the Reverend Clare in the long and short term then so much the better.

The ceremony was short, the groom radiant and the bride silent.

Mrs Flynn had dressed the girl in the prettiest of the new frocks James ordered made for her. It was pink—Willoughby had wanted white but Mrs Flynn insisted it would wash-out someone so pale and she had carried the day, on territory too uncertain for a male to risk insistence.

The ring was not a plain yellow band, but something different, white gold set with an enormous amethyst. She seemed to like the stone, staring at it throughout the ceremony, smiling at the parson when he asked if she agreed to the marriage. Willoughby saw only a smile but heard a resounding 'Yes', and convinced himself that she loved him.

She didn't seem to care what he did to her body—having no experience of men, either good or bad, having no concept of her body as her own, she accepted whatever he did to her. For his part, he laboured over her trying to elicit a response, some sign of love or lust, some desire to *be* with him. Never finding it, he became frustrated, at first simply slaking his own lust, quickly. Gradually, he became a little cruel, pinching, biting, hoping to inflict on her a little of the hurt his love caused him. For all the centuries men have dreamed of the joy of a silent wife, Willoughby discovered that the reality of one was entirely unsatisfactory.

It was Mrs Flynn who first noticed the changes in her. Not her husband who stripped her bare each night and used her body as he wished. It was Martha, with her unerring woman's instinct, who pulled him aside and told him the girl was pregnant. Willoughby became gentle once again, no longer insisting upon his conjugal rights, but sleeping wrapped around her, his hands wandering to the slowly swelling belly, praying that what he had planted there would stay, and would in turn, keep her by his side.

More and more, he found her under the jacaranda tree. She sat silently for hours, no longer interested in painting, but stroking her growing belly as if soothing the child inside. Whenever he arrived back at the house at the end of the day he would go straight to the tree, for he knew that was where he would find his wife.

"Where's Sally?" demanded Willoughby. On one of his infrequent trips to the kitchen, he found Martha alone; no sign of the indigenous girl (re-named 'Sally' in spite of her protests) who helped around the kitchen.

"Gone. They're all gone, all the natives. They won't come here anymore," said Mrs Flynn, her skin shining, hair trying to escape the cotton cap as usual.

Willoughby paused, astounded. "Why not? Haven't I always been good to them? I've never abused them or punished them unduly. I don't understand."

Mrs Flynn was silent for a moment, weighing her words, wishing she's not opened her mouth in the first place. How to explain? "It's Emily. They're scared of her," she said reluctantly.

"Scared of Emily?" His laugh was sharp. "How the hell can anyone be scared of Emily?"

"She's ... different, Master James. Leave it at that. It scares them. They have their legends and she scares them."

"What bloody legends? What are you talking about?" He gripped her upper arm tightly, squeezing a slight squeal from her as the flesh began to pinch between his knuckles. She could smell the sour brandy on his breath. He let her go, but insisted, "What legends, damn it?"

"Sally said they come from the trees. They don't belong anywhere. They bring grief and eventually they go back to the trees." Mrs Flynn batted away tears with the back of her hand.

Willoughby stared at her. "And you? What do you think?"

"There are superstitions and then there are things we cannot understand, Master James." She bent her head, new tears fell onto the dough she was kneading; she folded them into the rubbery mixture and refused to look at him again. He left the kitchen, swearing and shaking his head.

Willoughby rounded the corner of the house, raised his eyes and saw his wife, her curved belly seeming to defy gravity, walking slowly towards the jacaranda tree. She stood before its thick trunk and placed one hand against the rough bark. As he watched, the slender pale limb seemed to sink deeply into the wood, and the rest of her arm looked sure to follow.

With a yell, he charged at her, pulled her away with a force driven by anger and despair. She was flung about like a leaf in the wind. Finally settling, she stared at him with something approaching fear, something approaching anger. He was too furious to see it and he ranted at her, finger pointed like a blade. "Never, never, never. You will never go near those trees again. You will never leave me!"

He locked her in their bedroom, then gave orders to his station hands.

"Get rid of all the jacarandas. Cut them down, burn them. Destroy them all, all the ones you can find."

So all the jacarandas within the bounds of Rollands Plain were razed; he even sent some of his men to walk three days beyond the boundaries and destroy any offending tree they found there.

He let her out only when he was certain there were all gone.

Her scream, when she found the dead stump of the tree, was the sound of every violated, outraged thing.

Mrs Flynn ushered the child into the world that evening. Emily did not stop screaming the entire birth, but Mrs Flynn could not help but feel that the screams were more for rage, than for any pain the tearing child caused, for there was very little blood. Strangely little blood. The milk that dripped from Emily's nipples smelled strongly of sap. The child made a face at her first taste, then settled to empty the breast, her face constantly twisted in an expression of dissatisfaction.

Willoughby came to visit his wife and daughter, his contrite face having no effect on Emily. She opened her mouth and a noise came like that of a tree blasted by storm winds. Having not heard his wife utter a sound before, he was stunned; having not heard anything like this, ever, he was appalled. He backed out of the room, and retreated to his study and the bottle of brandy with which he'd become very familiar since his marriage.

Late one evening, a few weeks after the birth, Mrs Flynn saw Emily, standing slender and silver in the moonlight, motionless beside the stump of her tree. She held the baby at her breast; the child was quiet.

Martha was minded, though she knew not why, of Selkie wives, women stripped of their seal skin by husbands afraid to lose them, by men who feared them more than they could love them. She called quietly to Emily and gestured for her to follow.

She led her to a stand of eucalypts not far from the house.

Within the circle of gum trees stood a lone jacaranda, the one she knew Willoughby had missed, the one she kept to herself. The silver woman needed to be able to go back to her place or she'd haunt them forever.

Martha shivered. She was terrified of this ghostly creature, but she hoped she loved Emily more than she feared her, loved her enough to show her the way back. She watched Emily's face as she recognised the jacaranda, smiled, leaned against the trunk and a sound like a leaves laughing blew around the clearing. Martha backed away. She watched the woman's hands slide into the trunk, saw her move forward, then stop.

The child would not go into the tree. Her diluted flesh and blood tied her to her father and his kind. Martha watched as the pale woman kissed the child's forehead and laid her gently on the ground. Emily pushed her way into the tree, disappearing until the brown bark was visible again, undisturbed for all intents and purposes. The tree shook itself and let fall an unseasonal shower of purple flowers, to cover Martha and the baby she scooped up and held tightly.

Willoughby drinks; Mrs Flynn often pours for him. She is strangely disappointed in him each time he swallows back the brandy decanted by her own hand. Most of her time she spends with his daughter, who has her father's dark curls and her mother's violet eyes.

She is a quiet child, but on the occasions when her cries have a certain tone, a certain pitch, Martha catches her up and takes her for a walk, to the stand of eucalypts. Rollands Plain's sole remaining jacaranda will release a purple blanket no matter what the weather, and the child stares up at the tree as if she finds it very lovely indeed.

RED SKEIN

RED SKEIN

Once upon a time, there was a little girl called Matilda. Her hair was dark, her skin olive, and her eyes as yellow as corn. She lived in a small village with her parents and brothers. Some days she was industrious, working hard to help her mother around the house. Other days she would sit at the window and watch those who passed with the same stare men and dogs use to eye meat and women. No one quite knew what to make of her, but she harmed no one and was loyal and loving to her family, so the villagers tolerated her eccentricity.

Matilda's maternal grandmother lived in a small cottage in the woods. She had a reputation as a wise woman, a healer, and—if crossed—as an efficient caster of curses. Matilda loved to spend time with her grand-dam, who taught her herb-lore and told her tales of women who chose to be something other than their outsides might indicate. Matilda's mother did not like her daughter to spend too much time with the old woman, for her own mother scared her and Beth feared that in time her daughter would grow to be like the old witch. Then God only knew what would happen.

A good few years after her bloods started, Matilda was still unmarried in a village that paired off its females at a young age.

It kept them busy—rearing children and tending a house left little time for questioning. Matilda, though, was different. What had been tolerated as amusing eccentricity in the child, was seen as a streak of danger in a young woman.

At seventeen, Matilda walked with a swaying gait that mesmerised and bothered those who watched. For a girl as yet unbedded she seemed to know how best to affect the men around her, and even some of the women. Her attraction was effortless, like a scent that floated from her skin and tickled the nostrils of her watchers.

Village boys her own age would have liked to know what waited under her skirts. They had tried to find out; some had worked up the courage to ask her to walk out with them, but when she turned her yellow eyes on them, their cool depths turned the would-be suitor's knees to jelly and his heart to lead. Matilda smiled and walked on.

Her mother noticed the gazes that followed her daughter. Best, she thought, to take advantage of them, of the girl's beauty, of the desire she roused. Beth approached several families with the offer of Matilda as a wife. While no one was so rude as to laugh out loud, no one accepted. As the tone of her offer became desperate, Matilda's mother sensed pity in the eyes of those she entreated, shaking their heads and saying *no*.

Something about Matilda suggested she would not be easily quelled, would not go quietly to a bed not of her own choosing and, perhaps, children gotten on her and left in her care would turn out as different as their mother; a yellow hue of strangeness running in their veins.

Each time a boy faded from her daughter's side Beth's hopes shrivelled and shrank. They mingled with her fear and tasted of bitter almonds at the back of her throat.

One afternoon, she called her daughter to her. Beth's voice was harsh, with disappointment, with the fear that put a hard edge on her concern for her child. And failure—she could smell the scent of failure on her own skin—in spite of her best efforts the child had turned out too much like her grandmother. When she closed her eyes, Matilda's mother saw her daughter, living alone and strange in a cottage deep in the woods.

On this particular afternoon, she handed Matilda a basket of food and told her to take it to her grandmother. The old woman was ill, unable to care for herself, and Matilda was to stay with her as long as she was needed. If the old woman died, then Matilda was to come home and the men would go back and bury the old witch.

"Don't you care, Mother?"

Taken aback, Beth slapped Matilda so hard that blood spurted from the girl's nose. When the yellow eyes turned on her mother's furiously pale face, they didn't even blink.

Matilda wrapped herself in a red cloak that her grandmother had knitted. The wool was the same shade as the blood trickling from her nose; as she wiped the fluid away it settled into the warp and weft of the fabric as if it belonged there. She plucked the basket from her mother's hand and turned. Beth's voice stopped her momentarily.

"She's not how she should be. She never was, not a normal mother, not a normal woman. Nor are you." The yellow eyes flicked to her once more, amused, fluid, fearless.

"No. Not like you," Matilda said and with that the last apron string snapped as if severed by sharp, angry teeth. Matilda left, her hips and hair swaying. She did not see the outstretched hand reaching to pull back the words, nor the tears that ran down Beth's face.

The way to Granny's wended through the woods. *Stick to the path,* was the village wisdom. Don't leave it or you might be lost— worse still, you might be changed. Change was worse than loss; change meant you no longer fitted into your place, you couldn't be recognised by your kin, and that was the greatest danger of all.

A boy followed her. A little younger than she, but almost a man, and desperate to win the admiration of the older boys. The task he had chosen to prove himself was Matilda; his goal was amorphous. 'Matilda' encompassed a myriad of things: walking out, kissing, sliding a hand up her skirt, or perhaps something more brutal, something he did not dare name.

He watched as the red cloak disappeared into the woods, flashing in and out of the trees and undergrowth. He hung back until they were far enough from the village that any protests she made would not be heard.

She cast a furtive look behind her and left the path, stepped into the undergrowth and tugged on the tie of her red cloak. The warm wool slipped from her shoulders as she disappeared between two enormous tree trunks.

Swiftly he moved forward then saw, coming from the other direction, an enormous grey wolf. A male, in its prime, almost five feet tall at the shoulder, with grey eyes to match its fur. It stopped, sniffed (the boy was grateful he was downwind), then followed Matilda's scent.

The boy had only a small knife. He didn't like Matilda enough to risk his life for her; then again, her gratitude might be worth something. Hearing nothing more from where the wolf and Matilda surely must be facing off by now, he moved forward.

The first noise to come to his ears was the growling, low and hard. Next came a whimpering, a moan: deep, but female. He crept through the trees, his boot catching on something soft. Her cloak lay like a spill of blood, still warm from the touch of her skin, intimate against his hand. His eyes came to rest on the remainder of Matilda's discarded clothes and then on Matilda herself.

She knelt on all fours, naked and brown, her face against that of the great grey wolf as they licked and sniffed at each other. Then she turned and offered herself to the beast, shaking with excitement, whimpering. The wolf covered her and she howled as he entered her.

As the boy watched, hard and panicked, he saw fur sprout over her limbs, saw her teeth lengthen and her jaw distend, saw her yellow eyes slit in lupine desire as the great wolf laboured over her. Unable to stop himself, the boy rose. His movement caught Matilda's attention. She howled in fury and, with an effort, pulled herself from her mate.

The boy's eyes widened. He saw sharp teeth in a wet mouth, a white circle set within a red one. Saw the muscles in her forelegs tighten and bunch in the moment before she leapt. There was only sky above for the briefest of moments, then pain and a wet sound, and, finally, nothing more.

When the boy was still and bloody, she gave him one last shake. At this sign, the male, who had waited patiently, joined her and they ate their fill, as though at a bridal feast.

Matilda shrugged back into her human skin. She picked up her basket and her cloak and continued on her way. The great grey wolf loped beside her, sometimes pushing his head against her hand.

Behind them, a woodsman stumbled onto the remains of the boy. His distress was multiplied by the fact that he was the boy's father. He tracked the wolf's prints, noticing how they intersected with a set of human ones.

Matilda and her mate arrived at Granny's house. The wolf waited patiently, lying across the doorstep like a large dog while Matilda entered.

"Still alive?" she asked the lump in the bed.

Laughter answered her as she put the kettle on the fire. Settling herself on the edge of the bed, Matilda held the old woman's hand and peered into her face. Surrounded by hair that had once been black but was now almost white, the face was strange: thin, the angles more wolfish than human, the pale eyes tilted toward the sides of the head, yet beautiful in the same way as a wild thing. She looked weary but well and Matilda thought she would recover.

"Still alive, little sweet. What did you bring me? Some of your mother's broth?" He eyes greedily picked at the basket lying on the table. "Did she send good wishes, too, my daughter?"

"She fears." Matilda dropped her eyes, sadness that she had hidden from her mother showed there.

"She always has," said Granny. "Beth fears for you more than she can love you. Because you're different."

"Because I'm like you."

"Yes. Like me." She opened her mouth to continue but growling and shouting outside the cottage interrupted them.

Matilda put her nose to the windowpane in time to see the woodsman raise his axe and cleave her mate in two. She howled in despair. Her grandmother struggled out of bed.

The woodsman hacked at the body of the wolf, his sobs punctuating the slap of the axe in the wet flesh. The trees rang until the mingled sounds were absorbed into their bark, marking them as surely as age would.

The man stopped only when he heard the grandmother calling to him.

"Thank you for saving us," she croaked. She touched his shoulder and urged him inside. He blinked his eyes to accustom them to the gloom of the cottage. "But we didn't need saving."

"You killed my husband," said Matilda. She dropped her red cloak to the floor as her real covering made its way from inside to settle on her flesh.

In the autumn darkness, Matilda's mother lay straight and stiff in her bed.

Her husband's snoring stirred the air with a strange violence and she felt the urge to poke him awake, make him roll over, have him share her sleeplessness. But she had done it before and knew that it would earn her a slap across the ear, a casually bruising blow that would ache in the morning.

She turned on her side, facing the window, seeing the full face of the moon stare down at her. Beth could feel the pull of it in the tides of her blood and tried to studiously ignore it just as she had her whole life. Denying her mother, denying her blood, denying her difference. Denying her only daughter.

Matilda had not come home. It was three days since anyone had seen her. The remains of the boy had been found soon enough. When the party of hunters descended on the old woman's cottage they found the woodsman, Granny's white nightdress and Matilda's red cloak, smouldering in the last coals of the fire.

A wolf had gotten in.

No, more than one: a pack.

Had to be a pack to slaughter three adults.

Matilda and her grandmother had been dragged away. Their bodies were being kept in some lupine larder.

Beth knew better. Her blood knew better. Somewhere they trod worn forest trails, the soft pads of their paws soundless and strong, eyes bright and all-seeing, coats soft as velvet and warm as wool, tongues long, wet and obscenely red.

A scratching at the door brought her back to the sleepless bed on which she lay. She slid from the sheets, slipped through the few rooms of the cottage silent as a shadow. In the front garden sat a young wolf. Behind it, outside the gate, sat another, older, its fur almost white. Two gazes, both intent, both cold, held her. Briefly she regretted opening the door but it was a dried leaf of a thought, picked up and blown away as soon as it entered her head.

The young wolf rose and made its way down the garden path toward her mother. Beth, knees weak, sank down to sit on the stoop. The yellow eyes mesmerised her and the beast stopped in front of her. She lifted her hand, rough and red with years of toil, reached out and fastened onto the fur, buried itself deep into the warmth and texture. She closed her eyes.

Surely now, she thought, *surely now I am dead.*

Then the fur, the warm body, were gone and when she opened her eyes the two beasts were fading into the night, down silent streets until they found the woods. In her lap, Matilda's mother found a long red skein of wool, damp with saliva and strong with the scent of wolf. She wrapped it around her wrist as tears slid down her face, stinging like nettles.

THE
CHRYSANTHEMUM BRIDE

THE CHRYSANTHEMUM BRIDE

*He who tries to express spirit through ornamental beauty
will make dead things.*
> — From an 11th century Chinese treatise on Art

"See how the skin glows?"

"It's like a pearl." It is only his second day with Master
Wei, and once again the boy congratulates himself on being
apprenticed to this man. Li is certain his future is assured. "How
did you make it so?"

"Soon enough for you to learn that, Li." The old man walks
slowly around his pride and joy, nodding to himself and smiling
a private smile. His hair is silver, long, no longer pulled back in a
tail; he feels himself free of the constraints of appearance.

"This is a work of art, Master Wei." Li's eyes slide over the
object in question, covetous, amazed, a little afraid.

"Yes. Yes, she is very fine."

Mei-Ju studies herself in a bronze mirror. The handle, once carved
and intricate, has been worn smooth. It had belonged to her
grandmother, concubine to a local warlord. When the warlord

died, his wife cast Grandmother out with only the clothes on her back, the child in her belly, the engraved metal combs in her hair, the mirror and the jewellery she had sewn into her hems as soon as the warlord began to sicken. Mei-Ju has inherited her things.

Sometimes, when she regards herself in the highly-polished bronze, she sees a face not quite her own. It is older, more beautiful still; she thinks perhaps the mirror shows who she will become. She does not stop to think that perhaps it holds spirits within. After these occasional visitations, she seems different, subtly changed, lovelier than before.

Her family is very poor but Mei-Ju is very beautiful and very ambitious. She is sleek but a little plump; any spare food goes to her, to keep her beauty intact, for her family believe this is how she will save them. If she is lovely enough, a rich man will take her as wife or concubine, then, they pray, prosperity will flow to them, that emptiness will become fullness. This is their fervent hope in all the years of lack, all the years when the groans of their stomachs compete for attention, trying to out-do each other: *My hunger is greater! No, mine! Oh, be silent.* Mei-Ju thinks only of leaving the hovel, not of what her elevation will mean to her family. She believes that when she at last leaves, she will not look back.

Her skin is flawless, a pale yellow, like gold washed to take the harsh shine out of it. Her eyes are black stones surrounded by long lashes. She brushes her hair, which is ebony, a black waterfall and almost long enough to sit on. Usually, she makes her sister, Chen-Ju, hold the mirror for her, but Chen-Ju is out in the field and their father would not consent to having her play maid to her beautiful sister, not today when they need the harvest so badly.

Mei-Ju is spared physical labour—not least because her feet were broken and bound when she was very small; even then they could see how wondrous she would become, how her face would change their lives. Her feet had to be made to match. The concubine grandmother was the one to wield the large rock, to break the bones as her own had been and to bind the soft, crushed things tightly. Mei-Ju's shoes are tiny and plain, but she dreams of one day wearing something precious, something silken and soft on her misshapen limbs. She cannot run, and walking is painful and slow (one reason why she likes to have her sister on hand), but she knows her golden lotus feet will help her totter to a place she longs to be.

"The robes are very rich, Master," observes the apprentice. The golden dragons running up and down the fabric glare fiercely at him. Part of him regrets what some may well see as waste.

"Of course, Li. This is for the Crown Prince. It can be nothing less than the best. The Empress would not have it otherwise."

"Her son was away for a long time," the boy hazards, aware the knowledge he gains here will help him navigate the treacherous paths of the Imperial Court. He is from a poor family, but Li is intelligent and enterprising.

"True. For five years the Empress could not do anything, but when her time came, when she finally drove out the usurper, she brought her son and heir back home." Wei nods sagely, adjusts a sleeve. "Bring me the headdress, Li."

Chen-Ju hates her sister. Her own face is flat and plain; they don't look alike at all. Some days—all days, really—Chen-Ju would like to rake something sharp down Mei-Ju's face. Not her nails—she has none, for they crack and split and tear to the quick from her arduous hours of manual labour. Something else, then: one of the engraved combs Mei-Ju uses in her hair, perhaps. The combs that belonged to the concubine grandmother. Yes, they would do the damage nicely.

Chen-Ju used them once, wound her own hair up and twisted it thus and thus. She made her eyes lose focus and her face seemed softer, almost pretty. She reached for a hope of beauty, her soul stretched out its fingers, almost had a grip on something she had never known; then Mei-Ju wandered in. She wasn't angry—she laughed. She laughed so hard she fell over, tickled beyond words at the idea that her flat-faced sister might try to adorn herself, might try to find something lovely in her rough visage.

Clenching her fists, Chen-Ju had fought the urge to hit, fought the urge to disfigure. She, too, believed that the cost of a future would be paid in the currency of Mei-Ju's face. It didn't mean she hated her sister less, but it stayed her hand.

She swings the hoe over her head, the strong muscles of her shoulders and arms forged from years of work, clench. The tool comes down to split the sad earth with surprising force. She pictures Mei-Ju's face in the brown of the soil. It is not simply the pain of always coming second to her sister, for she is not merely 'second'—she is *last*. Her life is a race she can never win against Mei-Ju's beauty.

Chen-Ju will marry a farm labourer, another peasant. Her industrious nature and tenacity will snare a husband, a man who wishes his helpmeet to work by his side, a woman who will bear sturdy children. She will never escape hard work, her face will never elevate her beyond the mud of the field.

"The Crown Prince was hurt?"

"Beaten, yes." He fits the headdress carefully onto the perfectly formed head, secures it gently into the elaborate black coiffure. "Nothing I couldn't fix."

"The Empress must have been grateful."

"Bring me those rings, the jade—and the bracelets. Yes, she has been my especial patron ever since." He straightens, arches his back, sighing with relief as his vertebrae crack back into place. "When she gave me this latest commission, I considered myself most fortunate. Not that one—the one with the dragon swallowing its tail—bring that."

"I hear your daughter is a great beauty, Wu Tsian."

Mei-Ju's father nods, his heart barely daring to hope. The harvest has not been good; he never thought to feel so hungry. He tries not to let his desperation show as he looks at the old man whose silver hair floats around his face in a haze.

"I am here to negotiate for her hand in marriage." Wei's eyes flit around the stark farm, recognising instantly, after a lifetime of judging people at a glance, that this man will be a happy to sell his glorious daughter. The old man nods, a gesture Wu Tsian misses. This family will not starve again, the clan who asked for a bride will pay well. Whatever they give these peasants will be nothing compared to the bounty they will gain from a marriage with the Crown Prince, but to this small, ragged *herd* it will mean life.

They discuss terms and Wu Tsian does not waver, does not hesitate when the old man lays out the conditions of Mei-Ju's good fortune. When Wu Tsian consents, his heart aching at the thought of the price his daughter will bring, he invites the old man inside. Master Wei is gracious, he has been in worse places (was born in one), but not many. The girl comes when called, tottering, doll-like. His face breaks into a smile; he had not hoped for this. "Golden lotus feet! My friend, how wonderful."

"We knew she would be beautiful, that an important man would want her, so we made sure she would be entirely so." Wu Tsian turns to Mei-Ju, who looks on expectantly. "Mei-Ju, our prayers are answered. This man has asked for your hand in marriage—to the Crown Prince."

Mei-Ju catches her breath; it is more than she could have hoped for. Her grandmother, the concubine, trained her how to behave. She simpers, is modest, but flicks her eyes up, floats glancing blows at the well-dressed man who has come to rescue her. He thinks, if he were younger, she would be a wonderful diversion; as it is he congratulates himself on his choice. The Empress and her son will be pleased, as will the family who are paying him to find a bride.

The door opens and Chen-Ju and her mother enter. Wu Tsian is so excited he can barely express their good fortune. His wife weeps for joy and announces Mei-Ju must pack. Her daughter gives a haughty look—what is there for her to take from this place? She will dress in Grandmother's one remaining outfit.

"Everything she needs will be provided, wife of Wu Tsian," Wei interrupts, thinking that families should not leave each other on bad terms. "Do not worry. All her needs will be met in the Palace."

Mei-Ju's heart thrills at the word 'palace'. Chen-Ju's face darkens, twists. Her salivary glands over-produce and she wants to spit in her sister's face. But it will not do, she will be gone soon.

"We should leave now; it is a long way to Chang'an," says the old man. Mei-Ju agrees. She disappears into the back room that acts as their only bedroom, gesturing for Chen-Ju to follow, to help her dress.

Chen-Ju does so with bad grace, she is not gentle. She tugs at her sister's old dress, so worn it rips in places. Mei-Ju ignores it, stands still as Chen-Ju removes the silken robe from the carven chest. This Chen-Ju handles respectfully, grudgingly. It is one of the things (like her sister) she finds impossible to ruin, something always stops her, some kind of fear.

Slowly, she unrolls the robe and slips it over Mei-Ju's head, her fingers fumbling with the band-knots. Chen-Ju steps away, raising her gaze to the glorious glowing yellow of her sister's form. The silk, embroidered with lotus flowers, matches the gold wash of her skin. She is a Chrysanthemum Bride, surely her fortune is assured. Chen-Ju averts her eyes; they hurt. Something lands on the floor at her feet.

Mei-Ju's mirror. Chen-Ju catches sight of her own face in its polished surface. She folds beside it and begins to weep.

"The family who bought her?"

"Had no daughter, merely an over-abundance of sons. But they wanted ties with the Empress. They knew I had been asked to find a bride for her son."

"They paid much for a girl to pass off as their own niece from the provinces. Are you not afraid they will tell someone?"

"Who would admit to claiming a peasant as family? Who would admit to sullying their lineage?" the old man chuckles.

"They must be very ambitious."

"Very. Always keep some form of insurance, when you deal with the very ambitious, Li. Remember that."

"Yes, Master. When they finally met, Mei-Ju and the Crown Prince—did she like her husband?"

"Not really, no."

Mei-Ju felt as though she had held her breath the whole way to Chang'an, and the trip from the outer provinces was very long. She rode in the cart alongside the old man, never questioning why she did not have a wedding procession. After a few days the yellow robe showed wear and she could smell the journey embedded into the thick weave. She would, she thought, burn it when she arrived, when she was showered with her bridal gifts, when she had better. Grandmother's cast-offs were not worth keeping. Perhaps, though, she would send the old hair combs back to her sister.

Her mind flitted briefly, dismissively, over the rumours that had reached them in their care-worn village, of the Crown Prince's disappearance, of the stirrings it had caused. He had been in hiding, obviously; now he had returned and she was to be his bride.

When they finally reached the Palace, the old man covered her face as they rattled through the main gates. She was taken into the Palace by secret ways. He left her with three serving women, who bathed her from head to foot, scouring her skin with brushes until she glowed, washing her hair, anointing her with oils and perfumes until she felt intoxicated with the scent of herself. Her wedding robes were rich, royal red, heavily embroidered, long sleeved, delicately made. Her hair was dressed, held in place with combs of jade and gold. They hung her about with jewellery that had adorned empresses for hundreds of years, and painted her face, until she looked like a doll. Her lotus feet were re-wrapped in clean swaddling, shod with new shoes finer than she had ever imagined.

She feels weighted down by her finery but she does not care; it is a burden she embraces, a weight she craves.

When the old man reappears she is ready, her excitement sitting in her throat like a ripe plum. He leads her to a large, richly appointed chamber. On a raised platform is a bed and on the bed lies a figure. She approaches slowly, her eyes downcast.

"Meet your husband, Mei-Ju." Master Wei's voice floats up to her as she mounts the platform.

The Crown Prince has a pale, waxy cast to his skin. He is a beautiful boy, not much older than she, and in full wedding robes, golden dragons rampant on the red cloth. His eyes are closed and his chest neither rises nor falls with the motion of breath. Now Mei-Ju realises that he lies not on a bed but on a bier. In spite of the embalmer's excellent work, there is something about him that speaks of decay; he smells stale and dusty beneath the heavy perfume.

Mei-Ju backs away, her tiny crushed feet aching, her heart swelling. She turns to the old man, who is now flanked by two large men.

"*Minghun*," she breathes, her eyes filling.

"He has been dead for five years?"

"Yes, beaten to death by enemies of the Empress. I preserved him as well as I could during our time in exile, but the materials to hand were not the best. Still, it was all I could do." The old man sighs, adjusts Mei-Ju's jade combs. "When the Empress returned to power recently, this was the first task she gave me, to find him a bride for *minghun*. An afterlife marriage was all she desired for him—no parent wants their child to go into the darkness alone, unmarried." His voice is soft, pained by the idea. "But Mei-Ju screamed. She screamed for a long time, and fought. In the end, though, she was too frail. We had to replace her robes, and fix her hair again, she was dishevelled by her struggles."

"You covered the bruises well," observes Li, eying the skin around the girl's lips.

"Yes. She would not take the poison willingly, my men had to hold her mouth open, pour it in, stroke her throat like a cat to make her swallow it down." He points to the places where bruises lurk under the thick makeup. "There is something in the poison that seems to restore the flesh after death; the marks were very much lessened after she had breathed her last. I don't know why. Perhaps you will find out, when you take my place."

"Ah."

"Come. It's time for her wedding. The families will arrive soon."

"Did her own family know?" Side by side they stand, surveying their work, the bride and groom in rich red, youth suspended, lying on their joint bier.

"Oh yes; well, the father did. Perhaps he told his wife. The girl's sacrifice has made their lives better. They will want for nothing. One life for the benefit of many." The old man nods. "I think it was an easy choice. Come."

Chen-Ju keeps the mirror for a month, until the day Mei-Ju's face appears in it. Chen-Ju is transfixed by her sister's wild hair, red-rimmed, weeping eyes, her mouth in a constant 'o' of despair.

It is the day of Chen-Ju's wedding to a local farmer—the family's improved fortunes have hooked her a higher rank of husband. She has the mirror propped on a chest as she brushes her dull hair, pinches her pale cheeks for some colour, smoothes down her unadorned scarlet dress, when Mei-Ju fills the silvered surface like smoke.

Chen-Ju watches for a while, then wraps the thing in a piece of old cloth. She sneaks out of her parents' house, makes her way to a field and buries the mirror and her screaming sister as deeply as she can. Chen-Ju's heart lifts; she does not bear the burden of beauty and for once she is grateful.

FROZEN

FROZEN

They found a child last winter, frozen on a bench outside the community centre.

His mother, who was inside playing bingo and drinking tea, had left him to wait on the bench in spite of the freezing temperatures. It was her habit, to let him sit outside whichever venue she was patronising at the time, be it community centre, pub, Indian takeaway. She, I understand, lamented the loss of the social security income he had brought her; she'd have to find another way of financing her fags and lager.

The bench faces the sea, which at that time of year is grey and glassy—although not quite frozen. I think it a pretty sad view for someone to die with; cold grey water being the last image etched on your eyeballs. It doesn't strike me as a gentle death; nor even a hard death ... just a depressing one, a slipping away into a nothingness kind of death. It seems unfair for a young one to die so.

I used to sit on that bench quite a lot, before winter came and it got too cold. It's nice in summer but I didn't think I'd be able to feel the same way about it after the child. People lose their kids in all sorts of ways; it's the careless ones that make me angry.

It was a lovely summery day; I wasn't planning on going there that afternoon but my feet had a mind of their own, or my mind was out-to-lunch; any road, I found myself on the boardwalk, rocking from my toes to my heels and back again on the planking, which is fractured and split like earth that's gone too long without water. Being there was better than going home.

The bench seemed different. It took me a while but eventually I worked out that it was because it looked kind of blurred; maybe not so much blurred as—well, you know when you look into a mirror that's cracked and you get two broken images? Like that—like the air had cracked and someone had done a really crap job of papering over the split; as if there was a thin gap that you could see through if you stared really, really hard. I walked around the bench, rubbed my eyes and squinted, but it stayed the same. Then I asked a passer-by if he could see it, and that was a bad idea because didn't I get a look and a half?

From under the boardwalk I could hear the slap and wash of the sea, rubbing itself up against the pylons like some cheap tart. I walked away and didn't look behind me, didn't give that bench and its broken space a second glance.

But I went back the next day.

I could only see a quarter of him the second day, like a sliver of moon as it passes through its cycle. I sat across from the bench, perched on the railings of the boardwalk, feeling the sun lightly toasting the exposed skin of my legs and arms, so white and pasty from winter hibernation. I bought a purple icy-pole from the man with the little ice-cream wagon who stands at the entrance to the boardwalk and watches all the young girls when he thinks their parents aren't looking.

On the bench was a section of a child: just an arm, shoulder, slice of torso and then the leg; as if someone had left part of a display room dummy sitting there for a joke, only no one else could see it. The bit wore a winter school uniform, that dark navy wool that gets faded back when you're poor. And the little limbs shivered but I couldn't tell if it was from cold, or fear brought on by a lack of understanding, or just because of the cracked mirror effect of the air around the bench. Maybe it was all three.

I guessed he was coming back, but he didn't know it; didn't know why. Bits of him were creeping back and maybe he was afraid coz he thought he'd gone somewhere for good, but now—now he was coming back here. It's hard on kids: they go back to places where they've been happy or because they've got nowhere else to go; they don't understand that sometimes you have to go back to places to fix things, even if you don't know how.

I sat for the rest of the afternoon and watched but no more of him came through. I guess some of that has to happen at night, moonlight being so powerful and all. I thought about staying but didn't fancy missing dinner for something that might not be visible. Anyway, I had something else to do.

The pub was full that night.

There was a little group in the corner, mostly men, rough hewn, clustered around a woman. She was the one I was interested in; shiny in a frayed kind of way, hair the colour of a too-new coin; everything about her was kind of frantic: loud laugh, sweeping gestures, but her eyes were dead. Maybe they were like that when she got them.

She seemed to be having a good time, this woman who'd let her child freeze, this woman who laughed up into the faces of the men around her, promising everything and nothing. Or she was trying to convince herself and everyone else that she was having a good time. I wondered how heavily he weighed on her soul, that frozen little child. Would she see him if she went to the bench on the boardwalk? Just that poor sliver of him?

I followed her home. She took one of the men, the biggest of them. He held her upright as she staggered in her white patent heels along the cobbled streets. I didn't approach—didn't like my chances with that bearded monolith. I could smell his sweat and testosterone halfway down the street. I only wanted to observe. I wondered if she was hollow inside—if I tapped on her chest would I hear an echo? Would the sound travel across an empty space? When they stumbled into her shabby little cottage I turned for home.

In my shabby little cottage there was a room with a crib.

When I got home, I started to clean it out. Brushed the cobwebs from the corners, chased the spiders from their homes, wiped down the walls and found that, yes, you really could wipe just about anything off gloss paint with a damp cloth.

We had painted the walls blue, Swoozie and me, and the crib white. There was a rocking chair, too, white with an embroidered cushion my mum sent. I stencilled toy soldiers and trains on one wall, a feature wall just like my sister suggested. The curtains were blue, too, with little bears on the fabric floating against the window. It wasn't much but we did it with love.

Pity Swoozie lost the baby. Pity I lost Swoozie.

By the fourth day, he'd come through.

It was dusk when I got there but I could see him quite clearly. Hear him, too, as he cried, such a sad little noise. People walked past but no one saw him, apart from me.

I walked up to him and smiled. There was a beat while he considered me, then smiled back. I think he saw in my face that I'd been waiting for him for a long time. I held out my hand and he took it, only all I could feel was cold, icy cold, no real flesh, nothing solid.

Where are we going?

Going to see your mummy, first off. Then we'll go home.

I don't want to go to her.

I know, but there's something you've got to do.

What?

You'll know when you get there.

It didn't take very long.

I led him to the cottage and he pushed open the door. I didn't go in, just sat outside on the step, massaging my hand to try to get some warmth back into it. The woman was pretty quiet, only a couple of screams, nothing to bother the neighbours—in that area, people are so used to yelling and screaming that no one raises an eyebrow anymore.

When he came out he sat down beside me, not quite touching but close enough that I could feel the heat radiating off him, like a small furnace—the way kids are after they've run around the playground. And he was solid now, he was *flesh*. We sat for a bit, until I thought we should move along in case one of his mother's boyfriends should happen by and find the mess.

I like having him around. I might take him to see Swoozie some time soon, when they tell me she can have visitors. When she starts to recognise the people who love her. When she forgets what she's done.

THE HUMMINGBIRD HEART

THE HUMMINGBIRD HEART

The tiny bird lies quiet in my hands; not tranquil, but quiet. I can feel it vibrate against my palms and I think this is good, will be good for my purpose. I keep the fingers of one hand over its sharp, black eyes, and, with the other feel the detail of its feathers, the infinite intricacies of its design. I pray to the gods that this will work.

I gently place the bird into the cavity in my daughter's chest, into the metal chamber Philotas constructed for me. He procured the bird for me, too; I didn't ask where from, it's like no bird I've ever seen before. He called it a hummingbird, crimson-throated, beautiful, like a flying gem when it's in the sun; it is not native to Greece. There are many things not to ask Philotas; this is just one of them.

I quickly close the thin metal door to the chamber, the door engraved with my family seal and Philotas' initials as maker. I turn the key and hear the miniature locks clutching at each other, closing and sealing; then there is the sound of the hummingbird, fluttering in the chamber, in eternal night. It will not like the darkness.

I sit back to watch my child, lying pale on the marble slab. The flesh of her chest closes over, meshes before my eyes. I wonder how long it will take, for the bewitched bird's beating wings to move the blood around her small body. Philotas said it would take "some time"; "some time," he said as I lay beside him, my body covered in sweat and the scent of him. It was part of the price for this sacred service, the return of my daughter. It was not unpleasant, and I would do—have done—far more and worse to get my child back.

Nectar, he whispered to me in the darkness, a lover's secret. *I fed it on nectar, so it will never sleep, never die.*

So my child will never again die? I whispered, hopeful, yearning.

I don't know, he confessed. *Perchance the body will wear out and the heart continue to beat when all flesh rots; perhaps when the body is gone, the metal chamber will rust and the bird fly out, back into the light.*

The idea of the little bird trapped in darkness forever lies heavily on me. But to wish for its release would be to hope for my child's end, and I cannot do that.

I lean forward, rest my head on the fragile chest, ear hot against cool skin, and listen. There is the whirring of frantic wings, and the slow, sluggish thud of blood. My daughter spasms, her torso rising, her head still angled on the slab, her toes pointing in pain. I fall back onto the floor. Breath explodes from her mouth, and a black substance, thick as tar, is expelled, glistening, serpentine as it rises into the air, hangs for a moment, then dissipates like smoke.

Antiope turns her small head and fixes me with a wondering gaze. She chirps: "Mama?"

I gather her up and hold her tight, feeling her tiny bones. The odour of death weakens with each passing second. Her arms wrap around my neck and I can feel her breath on my skin. "It was so dark there, Mama."

"You're back now, you're here now, my love, back in the light with me." I don't think I will be able to let her go from my sight for a second.

She is my child, loving as always, smiling and sweet, but somehow not quite right. Her hair, dark as ever, seems to knit itself into a pattern each night, weaving closer to her head, down her neck, like braids but more complex, more infinite than any braid could be. I do not look too closely, merely run my hand across the filaments, wondering at their strangeness, at their familiarity. Her eyes were green before she left me, now they are black. Philotas, who still shares my bed, tells me this happens sometimes—that the time a soul spends in the Underworld can seep into their eyes, which are never quite the same again. But Antiope, he says, is young, very young, and it will not much affect her.

He gave me back my jewellery today. In payment, I had given him my dower jewels and my marriage gems, the bracelets, rings and necklaces my husband gave me in the years before he died. In the years we were in love, before he began to speak of spirits following him, urging him to unspeakable acts, before he took our daughter and jumped from the cliff tops into the Aegean. He hit the rocks and broke apart like an urn dropped on a marble floor. Antiope went into the water, fortuitously drowning, but otherwise intact. Fishermen brought me her body.

I am a young widow, beautiful still, my charms undimmed by grief; perhaps illuminated by it. Philotas is older than he looks but younger than I thought he would be. He is not unhandsome but few women will have truck with a man of his ... talents ... my need for him over-rode any qualms I may have had. He is a kind lover, a gentle man; I do not mind that he has my body as a playground. I take pleasure there, too, and he, it seems, is coming to care for me, in his own way. He is kind to the daughter he returned to me.

Antiope watches the world with a bright gaze, her head tilts to the side to follow whatever object catches her interest; she has an intense stare. For weeks she refused most things I put before her at the table and I feared she would starve until I found her in the kitchen one morning, eating crumbled bread, digging her hands into the great urn of honey in the corner and licking them with glee. Sunflower seeds, too, these she eats by the handful. She drinks water with tiny, careful sips, using her tongue when she thinks I do not see, to lap at the liquid in her cup. She loves the light: her days are spent sitting in the sunshine of the courtyard, or at the windows, she soaks up the last rays for as long as she can, then races in to me and begs me to light as many torches as I can, give her as much light as possible, for she is afraid of the dark.

I did not fear until today. Until I found her perched in the olive tree, which is ancient, gnarled, with branches that stretch high enough for my eight year old to fall and injure herself. I still fear for her body, even knowing what Philotas told me. I went into the garden, calling for her, and she answered me with a laugh.

"Mama! Mama, I'm up here."

She clung to the branches, her toes curled around the wood, her hands waving at me, her dress torn, dirt smudges on her face. Excitement poured from her and I was terrified. I yelled at her; she refused to come down until I was so afraid I became calm again, thinking *I have lived through the worst.*

When she came down I held her, rubbing my hands across her skin to make sure she was real, alive, *there.* On her back, I found nubs, bumps where none should be, the beginning of bone structures where her flesh should be smooth. I ran my hands over them before I looked. Lumpy little spots below her shoulder blades, one on either side of her spine, stared back at me. I sent her inside then walked through the cool corridors of my home until I found Philotas.

I stand before him now and tell him about my daughter, about the vestigial things on her back and wait for him to explain, for him to put my mind at rest.

"Ismene," he says helplessly. "Ismene, sometimes things happen that cannot be controlled. You took your daughter back, you defied the will of the gods. But the gods will have their wish, my love, one way or another."

"You promised me!" I scream at him. "You promised I should have her back."

"And you have, my love, but I am a mere mage. If the gods choose, my magic will come undone." His voice is gentle and I hate him for it. I rage at him and throw things until I have no energy to walk to my bed. He lifts and carries me. I weep until I sleep. He stays but does not share my bed—I wake in the night to find him slumped in a chair beside a guttering lantern, sleeping a wounded sleep.

I wonder, for a moment, what woke me, then hear again the humming noise. It's so loud it might come from a giant bee. My naked feet pad silently over the tiles, the noise becoming louder and louder until I can barely hear.

In my daughter's room the noise is unbearable, but it has not woken her. I kneel beside her bed and listen, my eardrums throbbing in time with the sound. Reaching out, I touch her chest and feel the thundering vibration of her heart, of the strange melding of metal and avian. I caress the purple line where the flesh is joined and find her bright, dark eyes watching me. She smiles and the heartbeat quietens until I can no longer hear it.

"Mama," she says. "Mama, I dreamt I was flying."

I cannot bear to be alone again.
I cannot bear a child-shaped hole in my life.
I take her walking along the cliffs.

The Aegean is the blue of hope. The sky burns. I have to squint to see my way along the path. Antiope's hand is warm in mine, sweet childish sweat drips from our palms, but I will not let her go.

We come to the bluff; the grass is soft beneath my feet, the air is salty-sharp. I sit on a rock and pull my daughter onto my lap. She holds me tight, her head pressed against my chest, and I look down at her hair. The feathers are obvious now, black with a crimson tint, her hair neatly morphed into rows of tight, tiny feathers. She looks up at me, trusting. Her small hands seek out my belly and gently knead.

"My sister comes," she tells me happily. "And I must go, Mama."

My tears are salt and she kisses them away, my love, my baby, my child. Our hands hold, part, stretch toward each other.

Then Antiope is standing at the edge of the cliff, facing the sea and the sky. Wings sprout from her back, wide, black span of feathers and sinews and bones. She throws me one last look then sets her face forward. The wings beat down, once, twice, then she is gone.

I watch until the figure of my daughter is no more than the size of the hummingbird. Hands pressed to my belly, I retrace my steps, and head for home.

WORDS

WORDS

She was a writer, once, before the words got out of hand.

She would read aloud what she'd written that day, dropping sounds into the night, into the sometimes balmy, sometimes frosty air. After a while, she noticed that the words seemed to warm her no matter what the season.

Her voice became stronger, so soon she could read for longer. The sentences took on a life of their own, prancing and weaving themselves into the shapes of the things they described. She was always busy concentrating on those words that stayed obediently on the page, but one night, something caught her eye. A flowing diphthong movement, the graceful pivot of an elision as they wrapped themselves around each other and turned into a small, pale pink dragon, which then disappeared with a slight pop.

She knew, then, that she'd become something other than a writer. The word 'wordsmith' had hidden itself away in protest against misuse about three hundred years ago and refused to come out. The word 'witch' appeared but she ignored it, thinking it best.

Her house and the house next door were quite close—you could look out the window of one almost into the window of the other. Three children lived there, two little girls and a boy. They knew about the words before she did, had been watching nightly for some time. Their parents had been pleased—indeed so relieved as to not be pricked by suspicion—when they started going to bed at the prescribed hour without protest.

It gave the children time to brush their teeth, struggle into their pyjamas, get tucked in by their parents, and for George to sneak out of his room, across the hallway into his sisters' and for them all to take their places on the edge of Sally's bed just before the writer settled down on the old green velvet couch in her living room. Rose would hand out the hard sweets, the fruity ones that could be sucked on for almost an hour before they dissolved into a sugary puddle in the mouth. Unless Sally crunched down on hers (which she frequently did); then, she would chew noisily on the friable shards and beg Rose for another, promising not to do it again.

It may have gone on for years, until the children grew sick of enchantment or the writer died or someone moved away. It might have gone on forever if it hadn't been for the wolf. The writer rewrote Little Red Riding Hood, which was Rose's favourite story and the one that frightened Sally the most, so when the wolf swirled into being in the middle of the sitting room, grey and shaggy and rather larger than the word-creatures usually were, Sally screamed.

It still could have been okay had their parents not been walking past the bedroom. Their father flung open the door before the children had a chance to get away from the window, before George could duck under a bed, and before the word-wolf had time to dissipate with a half-hearted snarl.

The parents put their children to bed, all in George's room on the other side of the house. They held a discussion. They went next door and knocked.

"We don't like it," said the mother.

"We don't like what you do," the father said.

"They're fairytales," explained the writer.

"They're not ..." hissed the mother, "not normal! Stop or we'll tell."

"Tell whom?" asked the writer. "And what would they do? It's a long time since the age of torches and pitchforks."

The parents didn't think this was funny at all. The mother rang the Neighbourhood Watch chairman, Mrs Finnerty, who was also on a Committee for Moral Hygiene (though no one seemed to know what that was).

The mother told Mrs Finnerty what they'd seen; she also said that the writer walked around naked a lot. Mrs Finnerty (whose husband had run away with a young nudist) found her doubts about the word-creatures overcome when she heard about the nakedness.

Letters began to arrive for the writer, insisting she desist. She read the first two; tore up the rest as soon as she drew them out of the letterbox, recognised the stiff, off-white envelopes, ripped them up right in her front yard so the whole neighbourhood could see. She threw the pieces into the air and even if it were a still day, a breeze would start up and carry the pieces of torn envelope and letter into the gardens of her neighbours. The ones that wafted to Mrs Finnerty's always managed to land on her doormat and spell out rude words. In spite of herself, Mrs Finnerty started yelling some of those rude words back, coupling them with 'witch'.

The writer kept reading out her stories, the word-creatures becoming more and more realistic, staying longer before the inevitable pop. She started concentrating on landscapes, too, and buildings, so small villages would spring up on the carpet in her living room, with tiny people wandering the cobbled streets, carts pulled by donkeys, vendors arguing with customers in the markets; and all making a tremendous noise for their size until they disappeared.

The police were called but they weren't sure what they could do. They (a fat sergeant and two thin young constables) spoke with the writer and she smiled and laughed and refused to stop. She wasn't disturbing the peace, she was in her own home, and as far as they were aware, there was no legislation against writing this way. To the disappointment of his companions, the sergeant reluctantly refused her offer of coffee and cake and went next door.

They watched from Sally and Rose's bedroom window, with the neighbourhood parents and Mrs Finnerty all crowded in behind them. One of the young policemen found the discarded bag of candy under Sally's pillow (where Rose had stuffed it on that fateful night), surreptitiously put one in his mouth, and sucked at it.

As they watched, the clock clicked over to eight-thirty and a chime sounded, deep and sonorous. The writer came into her living room, gave the audience a small smile and shuffled the papers in her hands, rather like someone preparing to give a speech at a hostile debating society. She wore a long dress, green and flowing—the young policeman sucking on his sweet rather hoped it was a bathrobe that she would discard fairly soon—and her hair was caught up and covered by a scarf.

She turned her back to the window and began to murmur; this evening she did not use her clear reader's voice to project the story, but the word-creatures came all the same. Fairies, dragons, wolves, striped sheep and tuxedoed bears, candy-covered trees, men made of tin and women of cloud, and finally, a door.

It was a perfectly normal door if a little ornate, dark-wooded and banded with iron engraved with stylised holly. It was stout and it stayed. The neighbours and police saw her reach for the handle and turn it. The door opened and they could all see hills, sky, apple trees, and a cottage with many windows, many rooms. The writer turned and smiled and as she did so they saw their children, twenty-seven in all from teenagers to babies, with Sally and Rose and George in the forefront.

The children waved to their parents and stepped through the door, one by one until only the writer remained. Parents screamed.

Soon, police and parents were battering at the writer's house. She heard the windows break, the wood tear as men as angry as bears broke through the door. She saw the young policeman still sitting on the edge of Sally's bed, his mouth slightly open, the candy wet and just visible between his lips. She stepped through the door and closed it just as the first parent staggered into the room.

In their rage, they burned the house, but some nights you can see shades and shadows dance around the big tree in the yard. And the young policeman comes by sometimes, to sit beside the blackened ruins and watch in hope of a door.

THE LITTLE MATCH GIRL

THE LITTLE MATCH GIRL

The walls are a hard patchwork of rough stones. In some places, there's the dark green of moss, birthed by moisture and the breath of fear. In others, there's nothing but black. Soot from the torches is so thick on the stone that I could scratch my name into it, if I knew how to write. The floor wears scattered straw for a coat, stinking and old. No natural light comes into this place; there's not even a window, the opening bricked up long ago so no one might flee. And it stinks; the waste bucket sits festering in the corner.

I haven't seen a mirror in weeks, so I conjure my face in my mind: pale skin, green eyes, black hair. Reluctantly, I imagine the marks of my stay: dirty smudges on the skin, the eyes red-rimmed, the hair a storm cloud of filth. I try to smooth the ghostly suffering away, try to see my young face as it was, but it's no use. I'm forever marked. I close my eyes, tightly.

In my hand, a weight. A matchbox, silver and hard. Inside are four matches with the power to show me the moments when my life turned, when doors opened and closed, and my path changed forever. I open the matchbox and strike the first match.

The First Match

My mother died at my birth, after cursing aloud the blood-spattered bundle that cost her life and her man. I never knew my father: he left when he found his lover beginning to grow round. My grandmother, strangely untroubled by her failure as an abortionist, told me how she drew me from my mother's death and wrapped me in cloth, crooning that she would teach me all I needed to know.

She taught me herb-lore and human nature. She showed me how to heal a rash, how to draw the blackness from a wound and how to identify the people who would help or hurt us. We lived in a series of tiny huts, in small villages in need of a wise woman, moving on when a potion didn't work, when a child died, when cattle stopped breeding, when a wife caught her husband looking sideways at my tall, handsome grandmother—and later at me. At least six villages in my life, but they meld together, like wax melting in the flames of a fire.

My grandmother also taught me that we all had a fate. *Some of us*, she said, *are water, but others are fire.* Then she laughed. *Only problem is, you don't know which you are until they come for you.*

But I knew. I've always known. Children of water are dunked, children of fire become ash. When they came for her, my grandmother screamed as they tried her, and tied her, and fed her to the drowning pool. She had already sent me away by then, telling me to hide in one of the bigger towns, a city perhaps, somewhere I wouldn't be noticed.

It was she who told me about the rule of matches.

The Second Match

I stand naked at the window watching the snow fall, white as mother's milk, white as my skin, white as bones. Clean and pale until it hits the street, then corrupted, greyed, darkened.

"Of course I love you," I say.

I turn to face him, to see his bulk distending the sheets. He is a big man, his belly like that of a pregnant woman, his cock at half-mast under the expensive linen. Tonight is a good night, a lucky night. I'm not on the street, in the snow, with my breasts icy globes and my hair hard with ice. I'm warm. The holes in my shoes don't matter. The tears in my dress mean nothing.

I give him a smile—my best and brightest—and move to the four-poster bed. My fingers as thin as matchsticks, I reach for the sheet and draw it away from him. He blushes a little.

I start at his feet, his toes in my mouth, then trail up his legs, my tongue leaving silvery saliva as it passes. Then the cock, the core of him, meets my lips and another match ignites in my mouth.

This is how I keep warm. This is how I stay alive.

No wishes to save me—no good fairies or bright angels to watch over me. Just the Little Match Girl with a cunning mouth and a tinderbox between her legs.

The Third Match

"I need to see you again."

His words were my salvation ... my escape from cold, dirty streets.

A man in need; a man who would protect what he coveted. A man I could hold with the firm grip of my lips and my fingers. A man who sought me out and settled me in a house: small, but pretty, with a handkerchief of a garden, and primrose walls. A man who paid my bills and kept the bed warm when he could escape his wife. A man who wasn't cautious enough when caught in the grip of the lust I roused in him.

His wife reported me as a witch—I had to be a witch to pry her husband away, didn't I?

They put me on trial. I admitted to nothing but giving my favours unwisely. My lover, my keeper, my protector, crumbled like a poorly-built wall. He wept in the dock, swearing I had bewitched him with my eyes and caressed him with my lips. He confessed what we'd done, said that I'd done what no self-respecting wife would. The eyes of the men in the court turned to me, bright with fear and desire, warning and want.

The judge was an older man, a serious man, a widower of several years. He was like the others and hoarded his desires like shame and his wants like sin. He packed them away in darkened rooms where they grew fat and lush as mushrooms, covered with shit. He said he would need to consider his judgment carefully. I was to wait in prison, yearning for my primrose walls and handkerchief garden.

The Fourth Match

The judge comes to me and each visit ends the same way—with hard flesh and cries, with slick bodies and heated breath. The last time is the worst as he pushes me against the wall, my face scraping against the stones, blood seeping through my skin. This is my judge, my jury. This is my executioner.

As he slows and shrinks, he says once more. *Say you confess, say you repent, say you will be a good girl, and all will be well.* I am silent. When I raise my eyes to his, he sees the dark blood on my face, and perhaps the shimmer of red behind my eyes. He raises his hand, scoring a mark on my skin, blood staining his palm. He backs out, whispering my name with a fear that makes me smile.

If I were a witch, I would strike him down. If I were a witch, I would fly from this place. If I were a witch, none would stand before me. Alas, I am only what I am.

I drop my gaze and see what he has carelessly left behind. A matchbox, silver and hard.

Now there's only one match.

The judge offers salvation if I confess. If I lie. If I beg.

I kick the straw into a mound. I pull the filthy covers from my bed and add them to the kindling. I stand on the small mountain of my unmaking. I take the last match and strike it. It lights with a spit and a crack, and burns merrily at me as I crouch, touching it gently to the tinder.

I refuse to be saved. I am the Little Match Girl and I will burn.

THE JUNIPER TREE

THE JUNIPER TREE

It begins with the tree.

Branches reach toward the sky; the tree is quite straight. Its roots, conversely, go deep into the soil and spread out, consolidating their hold on the earth, making their foundation unassailable.

It is the tree that watches over all. It was here before the people and the house, frosted brown and white like a cake; it will remain after they are dust and ashes. It watches and winds its way through their lives in much the same way as its roots wind their way into the soil; it is indelible.

The tree holds many stories, they lie in its trunk like age rings. Its memory is a long thing. Some years it sleeps, some years it wakes and watches and listens. Some years it remembers the lives it has given and tasted and taken ...

There was a woman, once, young and pale and very lovely. Her husband had thought a young bride ideal for the getting of heirs. A more robust girl would have been better, he knew, but her green eyes and dark hair caught him. There was nothing else for it but to make her his wife and pray there would be children.

He loved her dearly; she was frail but this did not stop his efforts to plant his seed. The man spent as much time riding his wife as he did his horse and to far less effect—at least on the horse he travelled, conducting business and growing his fortune. His wife, however, seemed to be a barren field, a bad investment.

The juniper tree stood in the back garden. The wife loved its spreading branches and the whispers it made when breezes sang through its limbs and leaves. Of the many gifts her husband made her, her favourite was the simplest. A swing was hung from the strongest branch and on summer evenings the wife would sit and swing, dangling her delicate feet as she hung suspended above the ground, dress catching the air and fluttering behind her. The tree spoke to her and it was words of love she heard, before her husband collected her and took her once again to bed.

One spring, when her husband was away travelling, she told the juniper tree of her fears and doubts, of the rigours of her marital bed and of a husband who loved her sometimes too much and sometimes not enough. She leaned against the trunk of the tree, its rough bark smooth under her soft skin, its lower branches seeming to stretch and enfold her. She sank to the base of the tree, curled between the roots and slept for some time. In her sleep she dreamt of love without pain, of gentle caresses, of a lover who took time enough to ensure she was wanting and ready.

When she woke, there were small tears in her skirt and she was wet as she had never been with her husband. Confused, she retreated into the house, throwing uncertain glances at the tree.

She did not mention anything to her husband. When he was next inside her she thought of spreading branches and the touch of bark, and clung to him, rising up to meet him as she never had before. He was surprised but pleased.

The wife began to glow and grow, and it became obvious that her husband had at last sewn fertile seed. They were happy— he would have his longed-for heir and she a respite from his attentions.

The wife grew still.

Her husband was travelling, increasing his fortune so that he would leave a comfortable legacy for his coming child. One night when they lay beside each other the wife said:

"If I should die, bury me beneath the juniper tree."

Her husband, startled by her turn of thought, but certain he would not have to fulfill his vow in the near future, agreed.

The child killed her. The daughter, pale skinned, streaked with her mother's blood, was handed to her father, who held the child tightly and named her Simah. The juniper tree flourished, new blossoms bursting forth, fed by the wife's fertilising form.

The man was rich, and loved his little daughter, but he was lonely. A warm bed and an obliging, soft body were the only things on his mind. When Simah was five, he took a new wife.

Second Wife had a child of her own, a daughter not much older than the widower's little girl. Second Wife loved her daughter with all her heart and vowed she would love her stepdaughter just as well. She did try (in her heart she knew she had tried) but every time her husband slighted *her* daughter in favour of *his,* it grew a little harder. Each snub was a prick and her heart soon became a pincushion of jealousy. She began to take her hurt out on his child, in tiny ways at first, then in larger, more bruising ones.

Simah understood only that her presence angered her stepmother. She grew quieter, tried to shrink so as not to attract the woman's ire. Without conscious thought she began to dim, to fade, until she was a tiny voice that seldom spoke. She would light up only when her father came home or when she played with her stepsister. On the worst days, she fled to the back garden and hid in the branches of the juniper tree, eating its berries, her face turned to the sun and the wind, taking in for a short while the breath of a place where she was welcome.

Second Wife's girl, Marlechina, was fond of her stepsister, and tried her best to protect Simah from the worst of Second Wife's temper. She watched as her mother grew into someone she did not fully recognise. When Simah entered the room it was as if Second Wife darkened. Marlechina did what she could but, ultimately, she was a little girl, no match for the dark worm that curled inside her mother.

When her father was away, Simah was fed less than Marlechina; her clothes became old and worn in spite of her father's wealth; no new toys became Simah's while Marlechina's collection spilled from her room like a flood.

Simah's father loved her in the casual way men love their daughters, affection without attention. And her father, as fathers are apt to be, was blind when it came to his wife. The domestic sphere troubled him not at all—as long as his belly was sated with tasty foods and his bed was filled with an agreeable softness, he did not worry about what happened in his own house.

On one of his trips, the husband sent gifts home ahead of his arrival. A large box arrived. Inside it, Second Wife found a beautiful necklace for herself, a pretty ring for Marlechina, and for Simah, ribbons and the biggest doll any of them had ever seen. It was almost as big as the little girl and looked enough like her to be a sister, with dark curls and huge blue eyes.

The children held their gifts happily and Second Wife looked, the one to the other. All she saw was the size of Simah's gift compared to that of Marlechina's—she did not weigh up the value or even consider that her husband had thought carefully in order to give his stepdaughter a gift she would treasure. She saw it as yet another snub. As she seethed, her own daughter spoke: "Mother, may I have an apple?"

"Yes, in the trunk over there," she answered. Simah, glancing shyly over the top of her enormous doll, risked a tentative request.

"Mother, may I also have an apple?"

Second Wife turned on the little girl, a refusal at her lips, then paused and nodded. Simah followed her stepsister to the trunk. The woman shadowed her.

Marlechina drew an apple from the trunk and skipped outside to watch the sun shimmer across the red stones of her ring. Simah leaned into the great trunk to reach one of the rosy red apples lying at its bottom. Second Wife grasped the lid of the trunk with both hands and slammed it closed.

The child's body dropped slowly to the floor outside the trunk, now as still as the giant doll. The woman opened the lid and stared at the child's severed head. Blue eyes reproached her.

Shaking, Second Wife picked up the body and sat it at the table, then plucked the head from the trunk by its dark curls. Using a long purple scarf, she wrapped the neck tightly so the head appeared to be connected. Only a little blood escaped from beneath the silk. Second Wife hid in the parlour to watch what might happen.

Marlechina skipped inside. She looked at Simah so still and pale at the table, her doll lying on the floor beside her.

"Sister, may I play with your doll?" Receiving no reply, Marlechina gently shook her sister, which provoked nothing but a head wobble.

"Sister, I would play with your doll." Once again, she received no reply and she frowned at her sister's unusual perversity.

"Simah, answer me! I wish to play with your doll!" She reached out and violently shook the little girl's shoulder. This produced a more startling reaction—Simah's head rolled from her shoulders like a pumpkin dislodged from a windowsill.

Marlechina screamed, and her mother, watching from the parlour, charged into the room, demanding to know what had happened. Marlechina wept as she blurted out the story. The mother looked at the sad little body and its severed head and began to weep. Second Wife steeled herself—she was, after all, a woman who had decapitated a child.

"No one must know what you did, Marlechina," she said. Marlechina shrank, fear and guilt frosting her veins. "Get me the biggest pot in the pantry. I will put this to rights."

Second Wife cooked her stepdaughter; she made a lovely stew, with plenty of vegetables and a thick brown sauce. Some of the meat she kept aside, to hang later in the smokehouse to dry. Marlechina stood beside her mother, weeping. Her tears fell into the pot; the salt of her grief seasoning the dish.

When the meat had boiled from Simah's tiny frame, Marlechina took the bones and wrapped them in a cloth. She carried the sad little bundle and the doll to the back garden. She hid them under a thick pile of leaves at the base of the juniper tree, and ran back inside. She did not see the earth move and shift, the doll and the bones sliding into the dirt as if swallowed, taken to a place of safety.

The husband returned, his belly growling as the odour of cooked meat filled his nostrils. Second Wife piled the plate high with tender flesh and he ate ravenously, not noticing that his wife and stepdaughter did not touch the dish, nor that his own child was nowhere in sight. He ate and ate; the more he had the more he wanted and soon the large pot was empty.

When he finally pushed back his plate he looked for Simah.

"Where's my daughter?" he asked, picking slivers of meat from his teeth. Second Wife looked meaningfully at her own child, and he shook his head. "My *own* daughter."

"She has gone," said Second Wife, her voice rough. "Gone to visit her mother's sister; she wanted to see her aunt."

The father grunted, disappointed and disapproving that his daughter had left without his permission, though a stronger imperative had begun to take hold. His belly filled with forbidden meat, he now eyed his wife's sweetly curved flesh.

He sent Marlechina to her bed and, almost before she disappeared from the dining room, he was on his wife as if he would eat her, too. Plates and pot were thrown aside as he lodged himself firmly within her. Second Wife thought her happiness complete.

The woman grew round.

When her husband was home from his travels, she would draw his hand to her swelling belly and run it over the taut skin. She was kinder to her own daughter, gentle as she watched guilt swim in the child's eyes and dark shadows grow beneath them.

But she did not say, *It was me.*

She found herself thinking of the dead child as she rubbed her belly, blinking away tears and wishing things had been different.

Marlechina thought of her stepsister often. One morning as she played beneath the juniper tree, she heard the most marvellous song. Looking up, she spied a magnificent bird, plumed red and blue and gold. The bird sang and its notes began to sound like words:

My mother she killed me,
My father he ate me,
My sister she hid me,
Now my bones lie beneath the juniper tree.

A shower of colour fell toward Marlechina. She reached out, grasped the rainbow, and found coloured ribbons in her hand.

The silk shone, glowing like gems in the sunlight. She looked up again but the bird was gone, only the ribbons in her fingers and the memory of its words remained.

She knew now that she hadn't killed her sister. She knew now that her mother had done it. And she didn't know what to do. She could only watch.

The father, returning from an evening at the tavern, staggered into the yard. From behind the house he heard a song, beautiful and gloriously lonely. He made his way to the back garden and saw a wondrous bird in the juniper tree. It sang him a song like none he'd ever heard:

My mother she killed me,
My father he ate me,
My sister she hid me,
Now my bones lie beneath the juniper tree.

Alas, he didn't understand a single word. When she had finished her serenade, she shook her beautiful head and dropped him something that flashed in the moonlight.

It was a golden chain and it held, banded in wrought gold, a small bone, like that of a child's finger. The man took it to be a religious piece, the finger bone of a saint, a piece of jewelry picked up by the bird in its travels, stolen because it was shiny. He believed in religion, not magic. He hung the gift around his neck and looked up.

She was gone; she had seen his lack of understanding and disappeared.

Second Wife, hanging out washing, heard the song. She did not understand the words but it sounded to her like the sonorous ring of funeral bells, and it struck at her heart with its pain and beauty. She thought of her little stepdaughter, of the way her head had rolled from her shoulders, and she felt pierced. Tears came unbidden.

The bird, glorious fair, swooped down and hovered in front of the woman. It drank in her pain and her regret, her loss, and saw the empty place where Simah could have resided had jealousy not taken hold. In the bird's beak appeared a juniper berry. Second Wife held out her hand and caught the berry as it dropped. With a flurry of feathers the bird was gone. The woman put the berry to her lips and swallowed, the bitter-sweet flesh and juice leaving their taste in her mouth long after the morsel was gone and she had returned to the house.

She began to crave the berries daily; they hung on the tree's branches, tantalisingly just out of reach, purple and lush. Second Wife stood, heavy and fecund, at the base of the tree and stared upward. The tree shivered and shook, and a hail of fruit fell upon her. She dropped to her knees and began to devour the berries.

When they were gone and her mouth was rimmed purple with their juice, Second Wife raised her eyes and the tree, sensing she still hungered, shuddered until she was once again showered with berries. This second feast sated her and she curled into the roots at the base of the tree.

The feasting became a ritual; no matter what she had eaten or how much, she craved the berries. In her final months they were all she ate, greedily sucking them into her mouth like a child at the breast, juice dripping from her chin. Gradually her hair began to darken and her eyes lost their blueness, hazing into green. Her skin, once golden, lost its colour even though she sat in the glare of the sun for hours at a time, consuming juniper berries. Her nature, once prone to blazing up, settled to a contented hum.

Marlechina watched her mother from a distance, from the windows of her attic room, fingering the ribbons in her hair, singing quietly.

She gave birth beneath the juniper tree. She'd woken in the middle of the night, pains familiar and strangely comforting, rippling across her abdomen. From the garden she could hear—ever so faintly—the song of the bird. She slid from the bed, away from her husband's snoring bulk, and wrapped a shawl about her shoulders. Her feet took her where her mind did not think to go, a movement without thought but necessary nonetheless.

There was no sign of the bird, but the tree welcomed her. She sank to the ground between its roots, and felt the pressure of a child anxious to enter the world. The smell of juniper berries was strong as her waters broke. The child came swiftly.

Marlechina, in her attic room, woke to the sound of bird song. She looked from the window. The white of her mother's nightgown caught her attention and she left her room, swiftly and silently.

Second Wife looked up at her daughter and wept. She lifted the child.

It was the doll. Simah's doll, streaked with blood and birth fluids, still, hard, soulless. Second Wife sobbed.

The bird perched at the top of the tree. In its beak, a juniper berry once again. It dropped the berry into Marlechina's waiting hands. She knelt and gently squeezed the berry between the doll's ever-so-slightly parted lips.

There was a catch of breath; the doll gasped and moved in her mother's arms. Her flesh became malleable, soft and warm as she squirmed, growing rapidly before their eyes.

Marlechina lifted the child, and found her eyes open wide, deep and knowing. Simah's eyes. The child became heavier. Marlechina had to put her down and within minutes the baby was no more. Simah stood before them, naked, and exactly as she had been on the day of her death. Except for the little finger of her left hand, which was missing. The sisters looked at their mother, now almost bloodless, but smiling.

"Take care of your sister, Marlechina." As the little girls watched, the earth beneath their mother's body opened and drew her down, to rest beneath the juniper tree.

SKIN

SKIN

I was sixteen when he plucked me from the sea.

Caught in his fisherman's net, I thought I would drown until he lifted me into the boat and began to hack at the rough fibres to release me. I should have known then how soft his heart was, to see him ruining a net so, but I was terrified. In his haste he cut me, split my tail a good eight inches and saw the fine-boned ankles lying within. He sat back, astonished, and I fought my way free of the pelt until I was naked and shivering in my human skin, huddled at the bottom of that little, little boat.

His family told him to throw me back, to return my other skin and send me home.

I learned his language and gave him children, two boys and three girls, all in the space of ten years. We were happy, for a long time, in our cottage on the tiny island inhabited by no more than fifteen families. They were all related, his cousins at one remove or other. And they were dark, some of them, so I knew they had selkie blood for all they thought themselves better than me. It made me laugh to see his mother come a-visiting, mouth all twisted like she'd sucked on something bitter, she with her eyes so black you couldn't tell the pupil from the iris. She'd look at my children, her grandbabies, and something in her face would soften as she watched them frolic on the seashore like pups. Sometimes she'd look out to sea and wear a longing that her mind didn't know, but her blood did.

We were happy until my man began to drink. I'd made him prosperous, for the shoals gather where selkie wives bide. His nets were never empty and the purse was always heavy from the sales at the mainland markets. The money it was, that led him astray. He would come home drunk, barely able to row across the short span of water separating us from the town, throw himself onto the bed and snore fit to bring the roof down.

When I begged him to stop he turned on me, called me *fish* and beat me for daring to question him. He was no longer the man who had saved me from a net.

I could have gone to the beach, knelt down and spoken to the waters, told the fish to go away. I could have pulled my old pelt down from the top of the cupboard where he'd hidden it all those years ago, as if I wouldn't sniff out my own skin. I could have taken to the water once more and left them all behind, but my children held my heart. My pride yearned though, for revenge, and I called up a storm just as my mother and aunts had taught me long ago; called it up one eve as he rowed home, worse for liquor and new-found temper.

They say there had never been such a storm and there's never been one since. I found him the next morning, when my anger burned low and regret took its place. He lay across the rocks, his clothes torn, his limbs broken. There was a skerrick of breath left in him.

I made my way back to the cottage, ran back down to the beach.

He was already very cold, limp, and for a while the skin would not take hold. When I began to despair it took a grip at last, adhering to his shoulders, down his back, across his chest and limbs, and finally up his neck and over his face. He coughed; it sounded like a seal's bark. Wriggling, he heaved himself out of my arms and flopped down the rocks to slip into the cold sea.

He comes often, not only when I sing. Our children swim as well as their seal blood allows and they play together; somehow they know it is their father, although I have not told them, and they seem not to grieve. Some nights, I sit there with him damp and warm beside me, and we speak of things beneath the sea, things I will never again see.

THE BONE MOTHER

THE BONE MOTHER

Baba Yaga sees the child from her window and knows that her daughter is dead. She bashes the pestle against the bottom of the mortar and swears she will not weep. The child is at the gate now, her hand nervously moving in the pocket of her apron. The old woman sits at the window to wait.

Vasilissa stares at the house. It is a tumble-down black dacha, somewhat forlorn in the late spring light. Chickens scratch at the dirt in a desultory fashion. A fence runs around the yard, and the gateposts are festooned with human skulls.

The blond girl shivers. Her stepmother sent her here and her mother, reduced to the tiny doll wiggling in her pocket, seconded the notion. She, however, is not so sure. Ludmilla, her father's second wife, means her harm but she is loath to think that her own mother has the same intent.

"Go to Baba Yaga and get us some coals for the fire," Ludmilla told her. Shura, her mother, said she should obey. "Ask Baba Yaga no questions she does not invite."

"Why, Mother, must I go?" Vasilissa had whispered to the twitching wooden doll. The thing had started speaking to her six months ago—five months after her mother's death, and one month after Ludmilla had married her father. She still doubted sometimes that the doll really did speak, but seeking out a priest and telling him the tale would be far worse than a little madness. Thus, she listened to the doll, who had never set her wrong.

"Because she is your grandmother, but she won't treat you any better for that. She has her own rules. Just do as I say and no harm will befall you."

Vasilissa had set out for Baba Yaga's compound. She walked a day and a night and on the evening of the second day she has come to the black dacha. A thundering of hooves splits the air and a torrent of air pushes past her, shoving her to the ground. She is familiar with the occurrence by now—in the mornings a woman in white charged past her, and at midday a fierce female rider in red did the same. Now, at dusk, a black rider takes her turn. She gallops past, through the gate, and disappears up the stairs of the dacha.

The little girl has spent the last hour sitting in the forest, watching the house, trying to ignore the tiny voice of the doll. At last the urging becomes too much and Vasilissa rises and drags her feet as she approaches the gate. The skulls glare down at her, eyes glowing red. She passes under their gaze, icy with fear.

Although she has been waiting for it, the child's knock startles Baba Yaga. She drops the pestle and it clunks heavily against the side of the mortar. From the air three sets of disembodied hands appear and she gestures for them to move the mortar back into a dark corner of the room, then she shuffles to the door.

The girl cowers under the Bone Mother's gaze. For the longest moment the old woman says nothing, just looks at the child, trying to see a trace of own daughter in the youthful features. Vasilissa peers with the same intent, thinking that the eyes set deep in the wrinkled face once looked out from her mother's face. A smile cracks the withered visage.

"What do you want, girl?" Her voice is the sound of the pestle grinding against the mortar. Vasilissa clears her throat.

"Please, Grandmother. My stepmother sent me to beg some coals from you. Our fire has gone out." Her feet are rooted to the spot as she stares up at her grandmother. Baba Yaga is tall and very thin, her face is a map of wrinkles, tattooed with age spots; she has a long nose and a surprisingly full mouth. Her hair is long and iron grey, pulled into an untidy plait hanging down her back.

"Stepmother? How long has she reigned?" Her heart trips at the idea of loss, of not knowing how long her daughter has been gone.

"Ludmilla and her daughters came to live with us five months ago," Vasilissa keeps her voice carefully neutral.

"How does she treat you?"

"As a stepmother does."

Baba Yaga grunts and steps aside so Vasilissa can pass into the parlour. The girl looks behind her surreptitiously.

"What, child?" The question is sharp. Vasilissa swallows hard.

"They say your house stands on the legs of giant chickens and moves around and around."

Her grandmother's bemusement is obvious. "Who would believe a stupid thing like that?" She leans down to the child. "When did you ever see a chicken big enough to support a dacha?"

Vasilissa giggles in spite of herself and steps across the threshold into a dim room filled with the smells of things that have lived for a long time. The doll in her pocket shakes.

After supper, Vasilissa watches her grandmother sleep in the big old bed across the room. Her face is less lined in repose but Vasilissa still thinks of each furrow as a journey taken, a map of her grandmother's past and perhaps one of Vasilissa's own future.

Will I look like her? Would my mother have looked like her had she lived? Is it so bad, to have lines to show where and who you have been?

Baba Yaga stirs, snores a little, settles. The little girl snuggles into the small bed she has been given and closes her eyes. Sleep comes quickly and she does not trouble the little doll for the first time in many nights.

They rise before dawn and eat a light breakfast, then Baba Yaga leads Vasilissa into the stable yard.

"Today, you must earn your keep. When I leave, you will clean the yard, clear out the stables, and sweep the floors. When you have finished that, take a quarter of a measure of wheat from my storehouse and pick out of it all the black grains and wild peas you find there. Then cook my supper." She leans down and whispers. "Or *you* will be my supper!"

The girl giggles, not in the least bit afraid.

"Yes, Grandmother. I bid you good day."

"My riders will come, my riders three. First is my glorious dawn, then my bright day, and last my tenebrous night. They cannot harm you, and will answer if you call." Baba Yaga climbs into the mortar, an ungainly scramble, grasps the pestle in her left hand and a long straw broom in her right.

The mortar, responding to her commands, rises in the air with a grinding sound and floats to the opening gate. Baba Yaga uses the pestle to steer and, with the broom, sweeps behind her to cover any trace of her passing. Vasilissa thinks it an extraordinary way to travel, when there are several fine horses peering at her from the stables. She shrugs.

When her grandmother has disappeared from view, Vasilissa pulls the little doll from her pocket. She puts a few crumbs of bread in front of the thing and a spoonful of milk.

"There, my little doll, take it. Eat a little, drink a little, and listen to my grief."

The doll shakes itself as if waking and eats up the morsels with alacrity. Vasilissa speaks once again.

"Today, little doll, I must clean the yard, clear out the stables, and sweep the floors, then separate a quarter measure of wheat from black grains and wild peas. Then I must cook supper. Tell me, little doll, what shall I do?"

"Cook the supper, of course. Leave the rest to me." The tiny thing jumps up and stands on the top step, raising her arms before she fixes the child with painted blue eyes. "Best you don't see this lest you become too old too soon."

Vasilissa bows her head and goes inside the dacha. She prepares her grandmother's supper, never tempted to look outside at the storm of activity the doll creates. Some things are best not known, some wisdoms should not come too soon.

The mortar makes it way through the trees doing surprisingly little damage. Baba Yaga knows her paths and, as she sweeps behind her, she ensures that no one can follow her trail, trace her back to the black dacha too easily. Not everyone appreciates her place in the scheme of things.

Baba Yaga is a woman who cannot be bound. She will bear no more children, she will bow to the wishes of no man; she is independent, adrift from the world and its demands. The world, in ceasing to recognise her value, has granted her a freedom unknown to maids and mothers. Only the crone may stand alone. She heals when she can and, when she cannot, she ushers others along their path, easing suffering, tempering fear.

The people of the forest know enough to leave signs when she is needed: a red rag tied to a fence or gate post. An offering is left, too, so as not to actually hand anything over to the old woman and risk the catching of old age, which some of them seem to think of as a contagion. She's a last hope to most, too feared to be willingly approached except in desperation. Oftentimes they wait too long. Mourners put such deaths down not to their own inaction, but to malice, to the crone being hungry to take a life, to feed herself on the juices of the living. She is deathless, strange thing that she is, and they assume she must feed off them to maintain this ever-life.

When she does manage to save someone, there is still fear—gratitude becomes a strange, haunted animal, constrained by a niggling unease, an idea, however unreasonable, that the price of her aid is too high. She should, she tells herself over and again, be used to it; inured to the ache it causes her. But she isn't; she suspects she never will be, and she fears for herself if she ever does become numb. Pain tells her she is still just a little human; something less than mortal, but more than a stone. This comforts, sometimes.

Today she saves a child and helps an old woman along the path, all in the same cottage. The child has a fever, easily quelled by a tea of herbs. She hands the child's mother enough of the mixture for two days more. The woman's mother-in-law lies quietly in a shadowed corner, waiting for the last darkness to fall. There is no request for her help with this one, it's as if the old woman is not worth the trouble, not worth an offering to the dark woman who roams the woods.

Baba Yaga sits by the narrow pallet, hands waving the hovering younger woman away. Her nose twitches at the stale smell of the old woman's body. She has not been bathed and she has soiled herself some time today or the day before. Baba Yaga looks at the younger woman.

"I hope your daughter treats you thus when your time comes. I hope she pays you the same respect, gives you the same dignity at your dying time," she spits and the woman shrinks away to sink against a wall on the far side of the cottage, hoping the curse will somehow slip from her skin, not embed itself in her pores.

Baba Yaga takes the hand of the old woman. The last vestiges of life have collected in her eyes, which shine in the dim room, and she smiles at the dark woman, grateful, for once, without fear. "Bless you, Baba. I beg you to help me pass on."

The deathless one nods and pulls a flask from the folds of her faded dress. She holds it to the lips of the woman, who drinks greedily. The old woman falls back and sighs her last breath.

Who would do this for me? wonders Baba Yaga. *Who would perform these things for me?*

The fact that she is deathless does not make the absence of an answer any less painful. She closes the old woman's eyes and rises, giving a final glance to the woman's daughter-in-law. "Bury her well. I will know if you do not."

The grinding noise of the mortar barely troubles her; she is so deep in thought that she forgets to sweep away the traces of her passing.

The old woman's son returns late that evening. He has been deep in the forest for almost a month and when he left his mother was hale and hearty. Her illness was sudden, occasioned by a summer cold and compounded by her daughter-in-law's neglect. His shock at her loss is acute.

His wife, afraid of Baba Yaga's curse and in full knowledge of her own culpability, seeks a scapegoat. She is desperate to stay her husband's hand, to keep his grief away from her, to keep him from ever thinking that she had a hand in his mother's demise.

"It was Baba Yaga. The Bone Mother came and took her." She does not mention that their daughter was ill, nor that Baba Yaga saved the child's life. She lets her husband believe that the dark woman took his mother out of spite, to extend her own life. He stays hollow-eyed beside his mother's corpse, sitting the death watch through the deep hours.

In the morning he buries she who gave him life, and when he finishes shovelling earth on top of the still form, he notices the path of broken branches and crushed grass left by Baba Yaga's mortar. Without a word to his wife, he pulls the axe from the block beside the woodpile and sets out.

Vasilissa, exhausted by her labours in the kitchen and anesthetised by the honey wine her grandmother had let her try, sleeps so soundly that she does not feel Baba Yaga's long-fingered hand slip under her pillow and grasp the little wooden doll. She does not hear the old woman shuffle from the room and shut the door quietly behind her. The child sleeps on, blissfully ignorant.

Baba Yaga, having eased herself into a chair by the fire, props the doll on a small table beside her and watches to see what the thing will do. At first there is nothing, no sign of life, but there is something about the doll that reminds her of a forest creature pretending to be a rock or a log in the face of a predator. She drops crumbs of bread into the small creature's lap and places a thimble of wine beside it. Her eyes gleam over the golden hair, the large blue eyes so like her own, and the full lips that, if her eyes do not deceive her, begin to pout at the extended scrutiny.

"There, my little doll, take it. Eat a little, drink a little, and listen to my grief." She leans forward, certain of herself now. "My daughter ran away with a worthless man and I did not see her again."

"Oh, Mother!" The doll jumps up and stamps its tiny feet, almost upsetting the thimble of wine.

"Ah! I knew it. You're a cunning little bitch, Shura," Baba Yaga sits back, shaking her head. "Not even properly dead."

"Dead enough it would seem."

"How did you come to this, daughter?"

"My penance for leaving you alone is to watch over my daughter as long as she needs me. In this ridiculous shape. Imagine my surprise when I died and woke up like this. Hoping for heaven or purgatory—at least—and this is what I get." Shura sits heavily and taking a deep draught of wine. "If I didn't know better I'd say you had something to do with it."

"Who's to say I didn't?" Baba Yaga runs a finger down one of the golden curls, seeing for a moment the little girl Shura had been. Wilful, selfish, demanding. Leaving her mother when she was ill unto death to go off with a man.

"Was *he* her father? The one you left with?"

"Of course not, Mother. Did you really think *him* the type to stick around?" Shura sighed. "Vasilissa's father would have had your approval. He was a rich merchant, kind and gentle. *Is* a rich merchant if Ludmilla's kept him safe."

Baba Yaga sits back and releases a pent-up breath.

"What's *she* like?"

"Like me, I suppose. She's looking out for her own daughters, but it's at the expense of mine and I don't like that." She looks down at her tiny fingers. "Truth be told, if I could kick her out of my bed and out of my house I would."

"But you can't."

"But I can't, Mother, no. You could, though. Or take Vasilissa into your own." The painted eyes shine as if alive. "You could do that, Mother, look after my beautiful girl."

The old woman's face collapses in on itself, as if her age has suddenly arrived with no warning, like a fat guest walking across a weak threshold. Shura watches as something liquid and silver makes its way down one of the furrows of her mother's face. This is the first time she has faced the devastation she caused. Her wooden heart, kinder than her human one was, twists painfully in her otherwise hollow chest.

"Don't cry, Mama. Please don't cry. Look after my child. Set me free." She regrets this the moment it leaves her lips. Baba Yaga's eyes snap open, turned to angry obsidian.

"Thinking of yourself to the last." She lifts the doll and holds it in her strong hand. If the doll could breathe, she would struggle for breath. "You want me to take your child so you can rest in peace. Then she can leave me when I need her, just like you did."

She holds the toy high, contemplating throwing it into the fire, stirring up the coals once more and watching the doll be consumed. Shura, sensing the direction of her mother's thoughts, is smart enough to shut up, to lie limp in the claw-like grip, and to hope as hard as she can that her mother's anger is not as strong as her love.

In the end the old woman simply shakes the doll in frustration, rather like a dog worrying a bone. Shura remains silent: she has retreated to her state of wood and varnish to ignore the horror of what her end could have been, of what her life may continue to be.

Baba Yaga does not leave the dacha that day. Vasilissa finds her in the morning, still sitting by the dead fire, motionless as a stone; although she breathes, her hands and face are very cold. She cannot move her grandmother from the chair, nor will the old woman answer her; the Bone Mother merely shifts her stare from the dead fire to the window that overlooks the yard.

Vasilissa brings cold compresses and drips sips of water between Baba Yaga's dry lips, but the old woman does not stir; her eyes have all the animation of glass. Vasilissa, fearful beyond measure, picks Shura up from the floor by the fireplace. The side of the doll lying nearest the fire is slightly burnt. Shura guzzles down the wine Vasilissa gives her first of all, finishing her meal with cake crumbs.

"There my little doll, take it. Eat a little, drink a little, and listen to my grief." Vasilissa takes a deep breath. "I fear my grandmother is dying."

Shura sags, a marionette whose strings have been cut. "She cannot die, but she can become a stone. She did for almost a year after my father left."

"What must I do, little doll? What must I do, my little mother?" To her distress, Vasilissa sees her mother shrug and shake her head. The child flares up. "We must do something! We cannot leave her like this."

"It's her heart that troubles her, not any physical ailment, Vasilissa." Shura's voice fractures. "How do you cure loneliness? How do you ease the pain of singularity? She stands alone. She stands outside."

Vasilissa gives her mother a frustrated shake and sets her on the mantle. She settles herself on Baba Yaga's lap, curling her child's form around her grandmother, wrapping her arms around the thin shoulders, burying her smooth face in the corrugated skin of Baba Yaga's neck. Her voice is soft as she makes her promises.

"Don't leave me, Grandmother. I will not leave you. You will not stand alone any longer. Do not become stone." Her voice strengthens. "I love you, Grandmother. I will not leave you."

She falls asleep, her promise still on her lips, sticky and sweet like honey. Her dreams, though, are fraught: she sees a man hunting through the woods, following her grandmother's trail, his axe sharp and his temper frayed by grief.

Vasilissa is woken by a noise in the yard. She looks out the window and sees the skulls on the gateposts, their teeth clattering a warning. Beyond them, in among the tree trunks, she can see someone moving, a man, with the late afternoon sun glittering on the edge of his blade. She grabs Shura and rushes to the kitchen, unsure how much time she may have while he stalks around the dacha, trying to learn its defences.

The little girl makes her offering to the doll and cries:

"There my little doll, take it. Eat a little, drink a little, and listen to my grief. A man comes, his axe sharp and bright. I fear for us all." She takes Shura to the window where they can see him clearly, standing just outside the fence, angry and uncertain.

"The black rider is coming, I can feel the earth shaking beneath her tread. Tell her to cast her darkest night over us and I will deal with this man. Be brave!" Shura exhorts her daughter.

Vasilissa runs through the dacha and throws open the front door. The man is inside the gate. When he sees her, he moves faster: it seems his anger will be spread over anyone he can find. Vasilissa can hear the beat of hooves and she shouts.

"Black rider, black rider, come to my aid! Throw your darkest night upon us!"

Her last glimpse is of the man tossed about by three sets of disembodied hands, then all goes black, as black as the inside of the deepest cave. She hears Shura's voice rising, chanting, calling upon spells of forgetfulness, of disorientation, to send the man far away, with no memory of the path to this dacha. For a long while all is silent.

Vasilissa waits and waits. She stretches forth and finds the doll lying not far from her hand, and she gathers Shura up, holding her in her lap. After a time (she does not know how long), the darkness does not seem so heavy and she hears a scratching sound and a torch flares. Baba Yaga stands at the door of the dacha and lights Vasilissa's way inside.

Baba Yaga takes Shura from her granddaughter and rubs a drop of water on the doll's lips, holds cake crumbs out for her.

"There my little doll, take it. Eat a little, drink a little, and listen to my joy." She says quietly. "I will look after your daughter, Shura."

The doll's eyes shine, her painted mouth moving in a smile. "Thank you, mother. My Vasilissa is faithful above all things."

"And when the time comes, Shura, I will let her go," Baba Yaga promises. "As I release you now, daughter. Rest."

THE DEAD ONES
DON'T HURT YOU

THE DEAD ONES DON'T
HURT YOU

The bruises were fading; pale yellow with just a hint of purple now.

There was the cut above her eye, still two stiches there holding the edges of the incision together. She would have a scar. Well, it wasn't her first; wouldn't be her last.

No, she corrected herself, *that was a negative thought*. She was *not* going to think like that anymore. No more scars. No more bad boys. No more putting herself last.

Melanie smiled at her reflection, careful not to smile so much that the chipped incisor showed. (That was a remnant from Joel.) Her hair was newly bleached, a sharp platinum; her eyes were small but a bright blue. Her best feature, Momma used to say. Unfortunately she'd generally follow up with comments about pug-nose, thin lips and flat face. Melanie shook her head until her mother's voice fell away. She knew it wouldn't matter to *him* but she wanted to wait before he saw her. First impressions and all.

The box was still where the delivery men had left it, in that little tiny space she liked to call the entry hall. She *so* wanted to open it but she was practising patience. When she finally did, she reminded herself, she wanted to look her best.

So, she wasn't going to open the box, no. But she could do some light reading. First, there was the magazine on her bedside table. The advert was in the back, right below the Singles Section. When she'd seen it her heart had done a little jig.

Life had seemed so empty again for a while—Cameron hadn't stayed that long. He'd gotten parole, spent two months eating her out of house and home and then taken off, leaving her with the souvenirs of his visit on her face. She'd been wondering what she was going to do, and there was the answer, just as neat as you please, in that magazine.

Given up on live ones? For 53 payments of $29.95 per calendar month an Ever-faithful Zombie Boyfriend™ *can be yours. Remember: the dead ones don't hurt you.* Then there was the owner's manual, which was even more promising:

Congratulations on choosing an EZ-Boy! Average guys too boring? Jailbirds too unpredictable? You have joined the growing ranks of women seeking a life-partner among the Walking Dead. Please read this instruction manual carefully. Failure to properly care for your purchase will render your warranty null and void. Remember: a cared for EZ-Boy means a cared for owner. Life was looking up. She smeared a layer of make-up across her skin, making it extra thick over the bruises, and began getting ready for work. She was on reception at 9pm.

Shaped liked a coffin, the box kind of creeped her out. Then again, Melanie reminded herself, she had just purchased a zombie as a life-partner so she'd best get over the squeamish. She picked up the crowbar and began the process of popping the top. It wasn't like she'd just bought a toaster or a TV, or something you could figure out as you went along, so she'd read the manual from cover to cover. No, this was an investment in her future. Now, as she pried open the coffin, the wood splintering along the edges like toothpicks, she felt anticipation zipping around her stomach like bees buzzing in a hive, busy and warm.

She flipped the lid onto the floor and looked inside. Well, he was handsome for sure. He looked like he might be tall too (she *had* ordered a tall one, after all). He'd short dark hair and she guessed his eyes had been blue once. Now they were kind of pearly, what with the whole patina of death thing he had going. His skin was a little grey—quite grey, actually—and yes, there was a kind of funny smell coming off him, like mothballs and something else. But he was smiling up at her like she was the moon. No man had ever looked at her like that before.

Melanie sat back in the banana lounge on the patio. She settled her hat firmly on her head and perched her sunglasses on her nose. Her tall glass sat on the armrest, a small circle of condensation collected at its base. Billy (that was the name she'd chosen for him) was mowing the lawn, shoving the old push mower around the yard, moving with a slight limp. She thought it might be a left-over from his life—his *living* life. He had no shirt on, six-pack in evidence, but showed no sign of sweat that she could see. One of the advantages of being a zombie, she guessed. She smiled at him and he waved and he smiled, mechanically, but nevertheless he acknowledged her and that was enough for her.

When she was at working at the resort and if she didn't have any chores for him, Melanie just told Billy to stay in his box. She didn't think he slept or anything, he just kind of powered-down like the computers at work when no one used them for a while. He didn't really have any hobbies; it wasn't like he was going to be a big reader or need time to finish his novel or anything. He cleaned the house like a dream, but how many times could anyone do that in the week? Day-time TV rotted the brain, she firmly believed, but had to admit that it probably wasn't going to trouble a zombie too much. She thought she probably could have left him some simple cooking to do but she was wary of having him anywhere near the salt.

The manual had been very specific about that—the type was even in a bold red—*It is important that you only ever feed your EZ-Boy the approved gruel formula (recipe attached), and under no circumstances add any sort of condiment to the mix—especially not salt. This will cause your EZ-Boy to return irretrievably to its grave and we must remind you that there are no refunds.*

So, no, that wasn't a risk she was prepared to take; she was happy to do the cooking, to make sure he had his gruel. He was *hers* and she was not letting him go for anything. She was going to be very careful with their future. She made herself comfortable and opened the magazine across her knees, so she could look between the glossy pictures and her brand new *boyfriend*.

"So, how does he, y'know, *do* it?"

It was going so well. She took Billy to parties. He didn't talk but he was attentive, smiled at her lots, listened as she prattled and filled her glass whenever it was empty. The other girls thought she was weird at first, some kind of loser who couldn't get a live one, but by the end of the night, well, that was just another story. All those women found that their live ones had drifted away, either to watch the football, or gather around the barbeque or the pool and drink and drink and drink until they could hardly remember their own name. Why, then her girlfriends were looking at Melanie in an entirely different light. That's when conversations like this occurred.

"Well, just the way the warm ones do it! But, oh, it lasts a lot longer," Melanie said in a confidential tone, enjoying the attention. "And he never complains about, y'know, eating at the Y!"

Dirty giggles all round, the kind of wolfish laughter girls made when they talked about getting the kind of sex they wanted.

"And so you say they've got a payment plan?"

She was willing to bet that more than a few relationships were going to end the next day and that *Zombies Inc* would be doing a brisk trade.

Melanie hadn't been exaggerating. Billy wasn't like the warm ones. He didn't seem to get tired. He didn't seem to tire of doing anything for that matter. She wasn't sure what he got out of their encounters, because he *always* had that slight smile on his face. And he never, well, *came*—just, well, kind of deflated a while after they stopped. He just kept going until she said "stop". If she didn't take charge, why, chance was he'd rub her raw. After she showed him what to do it was all good.

She found, for the first time in her life, that she was in charge in the bed. He did whatever she wanted. Sometimes, she got brave and experimented. Sometimes she made him be the girl—hell, it didn't hurt *him* and she started to understand some why men had done the things they'd done to her.

She also liked those days when she could put him in the bath and give him his weekly wash. It was just like he was her doll, so pliant, so obedient. The manual insisted he could be bathed only once a week: *Any more frequent washing will cause the skin to slough off in an unsightly manner. Your* EZ-Boy *will have its own particular scent. Do not try to wash the scent away—you will get used to it.* And she had gotten used to it. She never thought she'd start to associate mothballs with sex, but sometimes when she opened the closet in the spare room, where she kept the winter blankets and sweaters, and she caught a whiff of the camphor she'd carefully layered there at the end of season, why she just had to call for Billy.

Melanie found she had a lot of extra time on her hands. She could send Billy for the groceries, but she'd had to re-read the manual section on giving instruction because she wanted to get it *just* right.

Your EZ-Boy *is receptive to requests of quite a complex nature but you must be* very *specific about what you ask for. Loose use of colloquial language could be dangerous, for example "Take my hand", "Take your hands off", or "Keep your eye on something" could lead to an incident that may void your warranty.* She'd sent him out to do the shopping one week and then had to go to the store to find him. Melanie found him standing in front of the rows and rows of different kinds of cereal, pulling on his left earlobe that way he did sometimes. When they finally got home, she lost her temper. He couldn't show any reaction of course, no contrition and that drove her crazy—if only he'd said "Sorry". If only he'd been *able* to say sorry she wouldn't have gotten quite so mad, she wouldn't have started hitting him. She wouldn't have kept hitting him until her hands hurt. That's why she stopped; her hands hurt.

Melanie looked at the list she'd given him, later, and sure enough, she'd just written 'cereal'. It was all her fault. No point apologising, really, but she didn't want him making any more stupid mistakes. She wanted him to do *exactly* what she wanted him to do.

The woman at the reception desk looked familiar. Melanie gave her a bright smile as she checked the reservation in the computer. Yes, the woman had been here a few months ago—and again a few months before that. She'd always been on her own before but not so this time. "Hello, Ms Donaldson. Welcome back."

The girl next to her was tall and thin, with breasts really too big for her gaunt frame. She looked like a model, was dressed like one, except for her skin and eyes—the former a definite grey, the latter cloudy white.

"An EZ-Girl!" exclaimed Melanie before she could stop herself.

The woman's eyes lit up. "Have you got one?"

"An EZ-Boy," said Melanie quickly, anxious that the woman know she was *straight*. Melanie eyed the girl. There was obviously a high-end to the product, one beyond her price range—this one was *very* expensive.

Ms Donaldson followed her gaze and smiled; she ran her hand proprietally down the girl's face, neck, collarbone and then caressed the pneumatic-looking breasts. The expression on the beautiful, blank face did not change, but she gave a little, learned sigh. "Aren't they just fabulous?"

"Oh, my, yes. They are just fabulous. So well-behaved."

"Oh, and reliable and tireless! I don't know how I did without Felicia." Ms Donaldson smiled fondly, possessively.

"I've put you in your usual suite, ma'am. Roger will take your bags. Do enjoy your stay and let us know if there's anything else we can help you with."

"Oh, I'll be very well taken care of, thank you," she said.

The washing machine was broken when she got home and water had flooded the laundry. Billy was mopping it up. He'd used the machine lots of time before; she'd given him very specific instructions so she knew he hadn't done the wrong thing. He didn't deviate from his learned patterns, his accustomed rhythms, nor did he think beyond the orders given him. So, she kept her temper. They bundled up the washing into big bags—she only had one uniform left for tomorrow. The girls in the laundry at the hotel wouldn't mind if she threw a few things in with the guest loads.

Half an hour before Melanie's shift started, she and Billy waited in the alcove just off the lobby. Billy carried the bags of washing and they were waiting for the service elevator to the lower levels of the hotel. Behind them came the clip-clip of high heels and they both turned to look, nothing more than a casual curiosity on Melanie's part, and simply following a lead on Billy's.

Ms Donaldson and Felicia walked past. Ms Donaldson caught sight of Melanie and gave a conspirator's wave, smiling when she saw Billy. Felicia and Billy locked eyes, but neither Melanie nor Ms Donaldson noticed because they were too busy exchanging self-satisfied smirks.

Melanie left Billy in the laundry room. The girls were happy to let Billy sit there while the cycles went through. Melanie gave him a kiss on the forehead and went back to begin her shift.

A couple of hours later she looked up from plugging in reservations to find Ms Donaldson with a perplexed look on her face. "Have you seen my girl?"

"Sorry? Felicia?"

"Who else? I left her in the suite when I went to my meeting. Now I can't find her."

"Well, no, ma'am. I haven't seen her but I will let you know if I do. I'll ask around if you like, see if we can find her."

"Thank you. They're not supposed to wander off on their own like that!" Donaldson turned away, her heels making angry little sounds on the marble floor.

Melanie asked some of the busboys to look for the EZ-Girl and then figured she would take a break and check on Billy. When she got to the entrance of the laundry room, though, she found the Lucy and Susannah and Amelia crowded in the doorway. They were giggling quietly, craning around each other to get a good look into the room. Melanie walked up behind them, her soft-soled shoes making no sound. She peered over the shoulders of the three laundresses.

Billy was sitting exactly where she left him. Kneeling in front of him was Felicia, her head bobbing gently up and down as if in time to music no one else could hear. Melanie wondered how long they'd been going, if the EZ-Girl had the same kind of stamina as her male counterpart. She could hear a high pitched noise. At first she thought it was one of the machines in the laundry letting off steam, until the laundresses turned around and looked at her, their mouths o's of surprise—then she realised she was screaming.

She'd kept Billy in his box for two whole days while she decided what to do. She'd walked through her job like a—well, like a zombie—all the while her mind was on how to deal with the situation.

Melanie hadn't told Ms Donaldson. When she got her composure back, she just walked Felicia back to the suite and said she'd found the girl wandering in the gardens. They were booked for another week, so she figured she had time to think things through.

It wasn't that Melanie *hadn't* thought about telling, but she wanted to work this out for herself. She was going to take responsibility for this situation. She wanted to protect her investment.

And there was something else. Something else she wanted but couldn't bear to examine too closely for it would interfere with her view of herself. She knew it in her heart, recognised it, but wouldn't look directly at it. She wanted revenge, but she told herself it was justice. It was her right. But she couldn't afford to lose her job.

It took her two days of lurking, hours of re-reading the manual, carefully timing the calls from Ms Donaldson's suite. Melanie was practised at being invisible, she blended in like a piece of furniture that no one commented on, that everyone took for granted. So she was the perfect observer; the perfect spy, really.

She was rostered on reception with Davey, a young man with a large Adam's apple that drew the eye. Melanie caught sight of the food trolley going towards the elevators just after six. She casually picked up the pile of dry-cleaning (all of Felicia's model-wear and a couple of Ms Donaldson's suits) and gave Davey a nod. They weren't busy; this was the time when she did little tasks like this. The guests liked a personal touch.

"Hold the lift!" she sang and made it between the doors just before they shut. The room service guy gave her a big smile.

"Hey, Antonio, how are the kids?"

As she moved deeper into the elevator she seemed to trip. The dry-cleaning dropped to the floor with a whisper of plastic, individually-wrapped pieces sliding over one another, slippery as squid in a dish. Antonio bent down to pick them up.

Melanie lifted the metal lid from the bowl of Felicia's gruel with her left hand and with her right dug into the pocket of her jacket and scooped out the grains of salt she'd spooned in there before the beginning of her shift. The crystals shone under the fluoro lights as she sprinkled them over the gruel. They melted quickly into the beige-coloured mush, and she gently replaced the cover as Antonio stood, the dry-cleaning tidily arranged, the metal hooks of the coat hangers curved over his thick fingers.

In another day or so she'd let Billy out of his box. She'd explain to him again what he'd done wrong. She wanted him to know he could never do that again. She'd tell him what she'd done. She wanted him to know she was protecting him. Protecting her *investment*.

LIGHT AS MIST, HEAVY AS HOPE

LIGHT AS MIST,
HEAVY AS HOPE

"My daughter," breathed Miller, "my daughter can spin gold out of straw."

This sudden boast struck his fellow-drinkers as interesting, if stupid. Miller had a tendency to open his mouth unwisely when ale had passed his lips. The bragging was, however, astonishingly egregious. Their king, after all, finding himself in something of a hole, financially speaking, was wont to do anything to refill the kingdom's coffers. Those with wiser minds shook their heads; Miller was asking for trouble.

The Taverner, sensing the man was finely balanced between merely making noise and starting a fight, thought it best to send him on his way. He heaved Miller to his feet. The odour of flour that clung to the man crept into the Taverner's nostrils. It was the smell of his profession, of his world; had he been asked, Miller would have denied the existence of any smell. Miller swayed, peered at the Taverner, and raised his voice so that all in the tavern could hear. "My Alice can spin gold from straw," he bellowed.

Looking around, taking in the disbelieving looks with a bleary stare, he began to mutter. "A good girl, my Alice. Good, beautiful, industrious. Better than her bitch of a mother."

Noticing the three soldiers in the corner, the Taverner propped one shoulder under Miller's arm and manoeuvred the sot away. He felt eyes upon his back and sensed danger.

He sensed danger, too, in the way Miller spoke of his daughter's beauty. The Taverner suspected when Miller got that look he was somehow confusing Alice with her dead mother in the most base of manners. Sometimes he feared for the girl; most of the time he decided she was her father's property, like all daughters. And Alice was smart. She could take care of herself.

Miller stumbled into the night, muttering. A few moments after the door swung shut, a soldier detached himself from the huddle in the corner and approached the Taverner.

The sound of the front door thudding against the wall made Alice open her eyes. It didn't wake her, for she never slept when her father was out drinking, or when he came home, drunk and reeking of ale. She never answered when he came to her door.

At first he would scratch quietly, as if ashamed, then the knocking would grow louder, until he was hammering at the door and shouting, calling her by a name not her own. He would stay until he remembered who she was, and then sob for a while before going away.

For a whole month after her mother's death he stayed away from the drink. A whole month when he was her father and nothing more, not a monster or a nightmare or a beast. Weak, like all his kind, he succumbed soon enough and the visits to Alice's door resumed. Thus far she had remained safe.

A loud crash hammered her nerves before she heard Miller's voice, calling her down, calling for help. Tightly wrapping a robe around herself Alice unlocked the door and made her way downstairs.

Her father was crumpled near the kitchen table, blood flowing from a wound on his head. He looked up at her, pale eyes unfocused as they caught at her, taking in the tumble of golden curls, the eyes so darkly blue that they seemed almost black, the crushed strawberry lips and the swell of her breasts under the robe. He reached out, the gesture unfinished when he passed out.

Unhurriedly, Alice left the house to draw water from the well. When she returned, she knelt by Miller's fallen bulk and wiped away the blood, gently wrapped his head with a bandage, and turned away. His hand found her, kneading her thigh like dough, then clawing upward to her breast. She scrambled backward, falling in her haste to escape him.

He was asleep, but even in his sleep he craved her flesh. She took two swift steps and sunk her foot into his ribs. A loud gasp of air escaped him but still he slept; he would ache in the morning without knowing why.

In the safety of her room, the memory of her mother came to her with equal longing and resentment. Three months in the ground; three months Alice had spent evading her father. From her window, Alice could see the forest. Somewhere beneath the trees was the spot where they had buried her mother. As far away as Miller could get without exciting tongues; far enough, he thought, that she wouldn't haunt him and dog his conscience, far enough that he could forget her and take refuge in his daughter's flesh. His daughter with her mother's face.

Alice remembered her mother's face, thinner than her own, pale skin, bloodless lips, eyes bruised with sickness. A hand fluttering to draw her daughter close. Alice had stood back, believing her mother chose to go, thinking love was something corporeal that existed only as long as the body in which it resided lived. She refused her mother's final gift, her kiss, and ignored the dying woman who cried that she must pass a secret to her daughter. When her mother's sobbing ceased there were cold tears on Alice's cheeks. Angry and afraid, she stood at the door, refusing her mother's last kiss even as she lay: still, silent, and growing cold.

Now there was only her father, who watched her, day in, day out.

"Where's your daughter, old man?"

The uniformed men were impatient. Halfway between the mill and the house the four soldiers had reined in beside him;

Miller stopped in his tracks. His bruised cut showing a week's worth of fading, Miller was in no mood to argue.

"Alice, get out here!" he roared. Squinting at the lead soldier, he asked, "What do you want my Alice for?"

"Word of her has reached the king," said the captain.

"Who's been talking about her?"

"You, Miller. His Majesty was very interested to hear that your Alice spins gold from straw. Got all those empty coffers at the palace, he has. Maybe your Alice can fill 'em. And an empty bed, too. Maybe your Alice has something he can fill in return."

"Alice!" cried Miller as his daughter appeared, her cornflower blue dress and white apron very bright in the sunshine. Alice moved with grace, raising her eyes to meet those of the captain, ignoring her father as if she knew what he'd brought upon her.

"Your father says you can spin gold," said the captain, dark eyes raking her.

Alice eyed her father. Her cold contempt was unveiled for the first time and he shrank to the size of a child.

"If my father says so."

"The king has commanded you come with us."

"If the king says so."

"Is there anything you wish to take with you? Is there anyone you wish to bid farewell?" He shifted in his saddle.

Alice touched the small gold locket at her throat, then dropped her eyes to the thin ring on her finger. Both her mother's. All she needed of her old life. She shook her head. The captain reached down and she grasped his hand, swinging up behind him. The last Miller saw of his daughter she was clinging to the waist of the dark captain, eyes straight ahead, her rigid back the only farewell he would ever have.

The castle appeared like a faded starburst on the hill. The captain had told her over and over that the king was poor, yet Alice had been unable to comprehend a king with no fortune until she saw the faded grandeur of a palace no one could afford to maintain. They rode through the gates of a ruin as utter as her own.

Paint crackled on the walls as if to draw attention to its plight; anything gilt had been stripped; tapestries were threadbare; furniture was held together with spit and spider webs; windows, greyed with dirt, cracked under the force of a gaze. The crown jewels, once a wondrous collection of fiery gems, were reduced to a single crown, resting on the king's brow, set with a single diamond.

The king was handsome enough. Tall, muscular, black-haired and black-bearded. During her journey she had wondered if she might tell him the truth: that her father had lied. Perhaps he might find her beauty enough to stay his hand, but seeing this poverty she knew he could afford to forgive nothing. He would kill her and send the captain and his men to slaughter her father. While she had no objections to her father's demise, she had no desire to quit her own life.

Avarice and need ran through this man's veins. There was no safety for her here. The king's need for gold was a flood inside him and she would be swept up and drowned by it unless she found a way to negotiate the current.

"My father," said the king when the niceties were over, "was a spendthrift, and long-lived. In thirty years he managed to impoverish what was once one of the wealthiest kingdoms in the land. When I came to the throne there was just enough money for the coronation."

The corner of Alice's mouth lifted wryly. Perhaps he saw in her face that she thought the money wasted.

"Now my problems are at an end. Come." He gestured for her to follow him out of the dingy throne room, along a dimly-lit corridor, down chipped stairs, until at last they stopped at a wooden door, pitted and pock-marked, dark with age. "This should be no challenge for you, Mistress Alice." The king threw open the door.

From flagged floor to cobwebbed ceiling the room was filled with straw. Some bales had split and the yellow lengths spilt onto the floor like so much hope gone wrong. A spinning wheel sat, waiting for failure. Alice surreptitiously wiped her sweating palms on her white apron. The king caught the gesture and his smile broadened, dangerous and hard.

"You have one night, Alice. This night. Spin it all into gold and release me from my reduced circumstances."

"If I don't?" Her voice was stronger than she expected.

His eyes darkened as he drew close to her, his large hand slipping around her throat. He closed his fingers in a motion that was half-threat, half-caress.

"You have a very thin neck, Mistress Alice."

She held her breath until he released her and left the room. The sheer volume of impossible straw made tears heat the back of her eyes and she clenched her hands, digging her nails into the palms, hoping the pain would stop the panic. She was steel for a moment, before she threw herself to the floor, to the hated straw, and wept, wishing she could die on the spot.

Near her hand, one of the flagstones moved. She scrambled back in fright, almost burying herself in the straw. The flag moved again, jumping once, twice. A hand appeared in the crack between the stones. It was a small hand: white, smooth, almost feminine. It pushed the flagstone aside with surprising force as a man heaved himself up through the hole in the floor.

He was ordinary, so very ordinary. Not tall, but not short. Face round, unlined, not old but not young; hair neither blond nor brown. His clothes were neat, plain, and unremarkable; the kind of man she might pass in the street and not notice. He turned his eyes upon Alice. "Nasty."

She shook her head. "Pardon?"

"Nasty way to enter a room, nasty way to move about— under the floor. Always dirty and dark, especially in poor places like this." He brushed imaginary dirt from his clothes and looked at her again. "Fancy, a king with no money."

"Just fancy," said Alice bitterly.

The man's eyes took in the straw. "Straw into gold?"

Alice nodded.

"What will you give me to do it?" he asked.

She sneered. "You can't. No one can. Go back under the earth and leave me to die in peace."

"Rude, but understandable given the circumstances." He smiled a little. "What if I can? What will you give me?"

Alice looked down at her hands and saw her mother's ring. Better the thin ring than Alice's thin neck. She pulled the band from her finger and held it out.

"My mother's ring."

He took the ring and tossed it from hand to hand as if considering. His eyes were sly when he next looked at her.

"A mother's gift is very valuable. It holds magic. It's like a touch, or a kiss."

"How much magic has it brought me thus far? When my mother died she left me to my fate. If the ring buys me one more night of life, then it will have served its purpose well enough." Alice stood—she was taller than the man, but not by much.

"Fair enough," he said, pocketing the ring. He pointed to a corner of the room. "Go to sleep. All will be well."

"How can I trust you?"

Sitting at the spinning wheel, he grabbed a handful of straw and began his task. Within moments the straw had become gold, long strands of it, like wool. Alice felt its cold weight. She stared at the little man and nodded. "Thank you."

"It's business. Go to sleep."

Alice curled up in the corner, wriggling in the straw to get comfortable. Soon enough she drifted off to the whirring of the spinning wheel.

"Clever. Clever, clever Alice."

The king's voice woke Alice from a dream of her mother, slipping away from her. She sat up, noticing that even her pile of sleeping straw had disappeared, spun into wealth as she slept. Standing, rubbing her eyes, she pretended not to be surprised. The gold had been spun into thread and coiled into balls—unconventional, but legal currency all the same. She gave the king a haughty look that made him laugh. He called a courtier. Alice was to be rewarded: she could bathe, eat, sleep, take in the gardens, if she wished. She was to be dressed as befitted the king's favourite—in fact, she could do anything she wished except leave the palace grounds.

As the day passed, Alice noticed a great army of tradesmen trooping up to and around the castle. Repairs had begun. Hot on their heels were merchants with fabrics, gems, tapestries and all manner of the expensive frippery royalty are rarely without.

In the evening, Alice—bathed and dressed in new finery, her hair washed, curled and set with ribbons—was led to another room by the king. Inside was an even bigger pile of straw and the same spinning wheel. Her stomach swooped and her head spun. She wanted to weep, but made fists behind her back.

"Was last night not enough for you?" she asked.

"Thirty years is a long time to exhaust a fortune. There must be more. I'll make you a deal: one night for each decade. Two more nights, Alice, and your future will be assured." He stroked her cheek. "You will never spin again."

"And if I fail?"

"You still have a very thin neck, Alice." He kissed the base of her throat, just above her mother's locket, and departed.

Alice slumped against the wall and waited. And waited. And waited. After an hour the tears came, the floor opened, and her saviour pulled himself out of the depths once more. "Hello, Alice. Was His Majesty happy?"

"Ecstatic. Alas, he's also greedy," she lamented. Her hand rubbed at the locket, as if to smooth away any marks in the metal.

"This is a much bigger room, certainly. What will you give me tonight?"

"My necklace," she answered and pulled hard on the chain until the links parted and it came away from her neck.

"No hesitation, Alice. You are decisive."

"No, little manikin, I just have a very thin neck." She took herself off to the corner. "Do your work."

"Sweet dreams, Alice."

Once again the spinning wheel sang her to sleep.

In Alice's dream her mother wept quietly. *You're giving me away,* she cried. *You're forgetting me.* Alice put her hand out to touch the pale skin of her mother's face but the woman receded into darkness and left her daughter alone.

A hand grasped Alice's shoulder and shook her roughly. She started, and opened her eyes to find the king kneeling beside her, excited, stunned, amazed. He kissed her cheek and hauled her to her feet.

"Astonishing! Alice, you are really the most amazing woman." Cupping a hand to her face, he smiled. "Fit to be a queen. One more night, Alice. Make me the richest king in the land and tomorrow you'll be my queen."

He pushed her toward her chaperone of the previous day, with instructions that she was to be treated like a queen. Alice left the room, her heart heavy with the knowledge that one more night remained. She had nothing left to give.

"What will you give me tonight, sweet Alice?"

The little man's tone was amused and not a little cruel. He knew she had nothing. They stood in the biggest room yet, surrounded by Alice's yellow hell. As close to freedom as to death. There was nothing, Alice realised, that she would not do to escape the executioner's blade. One more night and she would be queen. Never again the smell of flour, nor fear of her father, nor planning how to escape the hole of her existence. For that freedom she was prepared to do anything. She fixed the little man with a determined stare and began to raise her skirts.

"You can stop right there, pretty maid. You have nothing I want. You're too old."

"I have nothing else!" she raged, tears streaming down her face. "You have already taken everything I valued. I'm a miller's daughter—what kind of riches do you think I am heir to?"

"Nothing, then. Only your potential," he mused.

"What do you mean?"

"Tomorrow you'll be the queen. He'll marry you, crown you, and bed you. Soon you'll have a child." He leaned in toward her hungrily. "I want that child, your first-born."

Alice rocked back on her heels. The glitter of freedom blinded her. She couldn't imagine wanting any child as much as she wanted to live. She nodded. The little man cackled happily, dancing a jig around the room. When he finally calmed, she pointed to the spinning wheel.

"Now spin."

"Indeed. Sleep, Queen Alice. Your future is assured."

Alice slept. She dreamt of empty places where mist and darkness reigned; her mother would not answer her calls.

The child had split her like a ripe fruit.

She lay in bed for seven days before the bleeding stopped and the physicians finally believed she would live. The child was a daughter, a mix of light and dark. The king doted on her. He doted on his wife, too; he had become fond of her and, through wise investment, had managed to increase the fortune Alice had made him. He honoured his promise never to ask her to spin again.

As she hovered between deeply-drugged sleep and wakeful pain, she watched him sitting beside her bed, the baby in his arms, making faces at the child and occasionally glancing warmly at his wife. She hated him. And the child; she hated the child most of all.

She didn't want to move, she didn't want to speak, she didn't want to feed the child, although her breasts ached with unused milk. She wanted them all to go away and leave her be.

One night she woke with a start. Perhaps it was the sound of stone scraping on stone, of a small man walking lightly to the crib, or the sound of him speaking softly to her daughter. She sat up with a sharp intake of breath as her stitches pulled. The little man stood by the crib, her daughter in his arms, his face alight with hunger and happiness.

"Thank you, Alice. She's beautiful."

"Get away from her," she hissed as he held the hated child. He made a moue and tutted.

"Now, Alice. Remember our deal." He approached her bed, jiggling the now-crying baby. Alice reached out, an unfamiliar ache uncoiling in her chest.

"Give me my daughter."

Reluctantly, he complied. "I will take her, Alice. In three days I will take her away from you."

"I will give you anything else. Take whatever you want in my kingdom, just leave my daughter with me." Alice thought her chest would explode. Was this love? Was this what she was supposed to feel?

"You have nothing else I want."

"Anything."

"Alice, you're not listening. You have nothing to bargain with. You had nothing after you gave away the last piece of your mother.

You forfeited her protection. The only thing you have of her now is your blood." He smiled. "I knew your mother, you know.

"Beautiful like you, but smarter. I offered her gold once, in exchange for you. She refused, but she was kind. Didn't teach you much, did she? Since I'm a fair creature, I'll give you one last chance. For her sake."

For a moment, Alice saw beneath his skin to a sharp-toothed, gnarled little beast squirming with excitement.

"What do I have to do?"

"Guess my name. Guess my name and the deal is void. You have three days, sweet Alice."

He clambered down through the hole in the floor and pulled the stone to cover his exit. Alice held the child all night, too fearful to sleep and too fascinated to look away from the tiny face that, mere hours ago, she could not bear to look upon.

"I have nothing left but my mother's blood."

Alice was out of bed, pacing. She would let no one near the child. The king was concerned. The ladies-in-waiting feared she would harm herself or the princess but no one could get near enough to separate them, and no one dared manhandle the queen.

It was the morning of the third day. Alice knew that as soon as daylight faded her tormentor would appear. She had neither bathed, nor eaten, nor slept. Alice had no idea of the little man's name. She had wracked her brain, going over his words, knowing there was something there, though she could not unravel its meaning.

She passed a table. Her robe brushed against a goblet and sent it tumbling to shatter on the flags. As she crouched to pick up the pieces, Alice cut her hand and began to weep. The baby began to cry, too. Alice lifted her daughter from the cradle. Blood trickled from her hand to the child's forehead, and Alice's attempts to wipe it away merely spread the crimson stain. Rubbing her own brow, Alice marked herself as she had her child.

She sank to the floor, huddling there, eyes closed, feeling the baby calm. Their breath slowed and joined; their shared pulse synchronised, a river of blood linking them, stretching back through time, mother to daughter. There, though, Alice sensed an end—a permanent ebb in the flow—an ebb that she had caused. She wept bitterly.

There was no sound, no door opening, but she felt a presence, a hand touched her shoulder, soft as silk, soft as breath. Without opening her eyes, she knew it was one who shared her blood. Her mother smoothed the hair from Alice's face. She breathed deeply, taking in the scent of her child and grandchild. A pale hand stroked her granddaughter's face and the child sighed, comforted. Alice felt her mother's lips against her ear and heard whispered words, light as mist, heavy as hope.

Wrapped tightly against the cold and tied to her mother's breast, Alice's child was silent. The rhythm of the horse's gallop was unfamiliar but she didn't complain. Alice had chosen the king's favourite hunter. A gigantic chestnut, he whickered when she approached, snorted in annoyance when she saddled him and rode him out into the cold night air, but he did not falter.

The sun rose just before they entered the darkness of the forest. Alice knew the path as surely as she knew her own heartbeat. Along the barely visible trail, between the two biggest trees, down the slippery slope, across the stream, then up the bank and on to the rise where her mother lay beneath a small cairn.

Alice dismounted, unstrapping the child and laying her gently on her discarded cloak. The cairn she kicked away before she dropped to her knees and, not having thought to bring a shovel or spade, began to dig at the earth with her soft, pale Queen's hands.

By the time she reached her mother, her hands were bloody, the nails broken back to the quick, and aching. The simple coffin was easy enough to tear open, the cheap wood soft and rotten from the damp soil. Tenderly she unwrapped the shroud she herself had sewn, her blood soaking into the fabric. She saw her mother's hands, crossed on her chest, the dark dress she had been buried in, and, finally, her mother's face.

Even thinner than before, eyes sunken beneath their lids, a white mould covering the once-smooth skin, but it was her mother's face. And the one gift she had not accepted still resided there. Without hesitation, without disgust, with nothing but love, Alice leaned forward and kissed her mother's cold, damp lips.

A breath passed between them and, in that breath, a word, and in that word, salvation.

Back in her apartments she sat in a chair, the child on her lap, both of them still wearing their blood. Eyes closed, Alice felt the sun disappearing, like a slowing pulse. A cold breath, as something from under the earth gathered around them. Opening her eyes, she found him crouched not far from her, grinning.

"You've made a mess. I shall have to give her a bath. Yes, that's the first thing we'll do when we get home. I'll give my little princess a bath."

"No."

"Still think you can win? Your daughter's flesh is mine now. No one above ground knows my name, sweet Alice."

"No," she agreed. "But those who sleep in the earth know. The dead know."

He stood suddenly, almost losing his balance. Alice rose, too, her grace restored. The child rested quietly, safe in her mother's arms.

"You weren't quite right. There wasn't only my mother's blood left to me. But a kiss *is* a gift. It was enough, Rumpelstiltzkin."

He screamed. He raged. But he could not come near her. He stamped his foot and it cracked the stones. He stamped again and wider cracks ran across the floor, almost to where Alice stood. He jumped up and down with such force that the floor erupted, showering Alice with shards of stone. She turned away, barely in time, to cover the child. Her back was pitted with rock, and blood dripped from her cheek where flying flint had made a wide cut.

When at last she turned back, he was gone. The hole was large, the edges scorched black and the shattered stones jagged as teeth in a dead mouth. Pain crept across Alice's flesh. She would be scarred but he was gone. And her daughter was safe.

DRESSES, THREE

DRESSES, THREE

I live, now, in one room.

The rest of the huge house is quiet around me; nothing runs along its artery-like corridors, no life. Perhaps that is why it seems to be dying. There is only me and I have taken up residence in the library, napping on the once-resplendent but now lumpen couch when sleep will no longer be denied. I bathe once a week, just before the woman from the village, who comes to 'do' for me, arrives. I, myself, don't find the smell of an aging man offensive, but Mrs Morgan made it clear *she* did, so for her sake I weekly wake the plumbing, and the pipes screech their protest. The water runs pale russet into the claw-footed bathtub; I lower my carcass down, and splash about in the lukewarm fluid for a time, like an ancient bird.

Mrs Morgan does the laundry, tidies the house, and dusts the furniture with such enthusiasm that some days I fear she will dust me if I stay in one place too long. She admires the many, many pieces of fancywork, embroidery, doilies, runners, littering the house. She makes enough meals for a week. I feed most of it to the stray, once-scrawny cat who is now very fine indeed, fat, shiny, contented. It's not that I don't like her cooking, but why feed a body that has no desire to go on?

Over the past months, I have moved methodically through the house, gathering all the bits-and-bobs pertaining to my life: reacquainting myself with them, reminiscing and, finally, systematically destroying them in the library fireplace.

I found, this morning, the last of the oddments to which my memories cling. From the upended envelope floated a peacock feather; a pair of butterfly wings; and a piece of paper, a list of words embedded into its onion-skin fineness with a calligraphy pen, traced in a very fine hand. Three things, three things upon which once hung life, freedom, and quite possibly a soul.

Finn watches his mother, her head bent over a piece of fabric; a paper-thin woman, and not quite right. Cerridwen has white fluff-hair that belies her youth, and pale blue eyes; she barely strings two words together, but sings in a sweet, sad voice that doesn't seem to belong to her. Her sole skill, her only resource, is her talent as seamstress. Cerridwen can spin a dress from air and spider silk if need be, and this is how she keeps them fed, clothed and housed. They do not travel by her volition, but are passed from hand to hand by rich women, wives of mighty men who can afford their helpmeets' expensive tastes for exotic frocks. The women offer each other ridiculous bribes for use of Cerridwen; she is, essentially, *purchased*. The boy wonders, some days, if she wishes for freedom, either for herself or for him, for a chance to not be passed from hand to hand like a strange pet.

He remembers no other kind of life, having been born into the erratic flow of his mother's travels. They have always been in 'big houses', she sewing and he wandering through halls and wings, attics and cellars. An old governess in the big house before last, freed of nursery duties and with time on her hands, taught him to read, and so he added libraries to his stock of places to haunt.

Cerridwen is eighteen when they come to the De Freitas townhouse in Russell Square; the boy, Finn, is nudging seven. They are installed in an attic room that is better than it should be for an itinerant seamstress and her fatherless son: the room is wide and high with tall windows through which pours pure white light. There are two feather beds, three trunks for clothes (they need only one), a place to wash up, and a large multicoloured Turkish rug, like a fallen stained-glass window, on the floor to keep the cold out of the bare boards.

Finn and Cerridwen come when Aurora De Freitas turns seventeen. One of her great-aunts hands them on—Aurora had demanded three special dresses for her Season and no one but the little Welsh seamstress could create them. Cerridwen makes sure she and Finn stay out of sight, sticking to their rooms as much as possible. Sometimes Finn slips away to explore when his mother is caught up in her work, her mind elsewhere.

Aurora De Freitas is different from other women. In fact, she simply strikes Finn as being not quite like anyone else, female or male. She has long black hair, straight and sleek as an Oriental, and heavy-lidded, slanted, pale green eyes. She does not walk, glide, prance, dance, or float; Aurora stalks. She has the gait of a hunting animal and a habit of flicking her eyes side to side, so she never misses a thing. It will be many years before it occurs to Finn that this was a survival mechanism. She is tall and straight-backed, but fine-boned and pale.

Aurora lives with her guardian, Master Justin De Freitas, a paternal uncle. They are in the Russell Square house for the Season; for the rest of the year, they reside in a grey stone manor down in Kent. Master Justin is obsessed with his niece. A portrait of Aurora's mother, Celeste, hangs in the library; Aurora looks very like her and one wonders if the obsession has merely been transferred from mother to daughter. Finn hears the whispers of the scullery maids that, although Master Justin has kept her to himself in the grey stone house, he has held himself in check. But she is seventeen now and has demanded a Season. They mutter darkly as they conjecture how she convinced him, what she promised him, how he will be rewarded after her time in London. He would never, everyone knew, let her leave him and marry.

Master Justin is not an ugly man. On the contrary, he shares Aurora's intense beauty, the raven-black hair and pale skin, but his eyes are darkest blue. His niece is the same height as him, and perhaps this has contributed to his patience, his caution: the fact that she is not a tiny girl who can be easily overcome. Perhaps it is important to him that she surrender.

They whisper that she does not lock her doors at night, but sometimes, when sleep does not come, Finn wanders the shadowed corridors and finds Justin at her door, whispering at the heavy wood, trying to convince her to let him in, let him in, only for a moment, only for a hug, a sweet avuncular kiss, only to smell the lavender of her hair, to feel its silk against his palm, only for a moment and then he will leave her in peace.

She does not open the door, at least not on the nights when Finn watches from the darkness, tucked behind a suit of armor, an old chair or chest, the long velvet curtains. She does not answer her uncle, merely lets him chew on her silence until he leaves, empty-handed, empty-hearted.

"You worked for my mother, didn't you?" Aurora's voice, if a voice could be said to do so, stalks the listener. Cerridwen dips her head but does not answer. Aurora continues, "Seven years ago, was it not?" Her eyes flick to Finn, sitting on the edge of his bed, legs swinging, shadowy blue eyes fixed on her; she takes in his tousled black hair.

Cerridwen says nothing except, "What kind of dresses would you like, miss?"

"The first dress—and understand this, I must have precisely the dresses I ask for or my bargain will not be fulfilled." She waits until Cerridwen nods her slight bobbing nod. "And so, I will make a bargain with you. If you give me exactly what I ask for, I will give you your freedom. A house, money, everything to live and you will never need to sew again."

Cerridwen's eyes are wide and she forgets to hide behind her dullard's stare. Finn ponders his mother, knowing she's not as fey or as stupid as people think. He wonders how she can bear to be thought of this way.

Aurora smiles and nods. "So."

The first dress she demands is to be made of peacock feathers. Aurora cares not at all for the design, only that it be made of the specified feathers. Cerridwen, who never sketches anything, never uses a pattern, sees the dress in her mind, finds it fully formed. She does not take Aurora's measurements; she has seen the girl and that will be sufficient.

The dress lies like a second skin. The eyes of the peacock feathers are everywhere; they bow and sway, viewing everything around them, seeming to move even when Aurora is still. Above her head soars a great spray of feathers, the fan of a peacock's tail, stitched just above the curve of her buttocks and just below the small of her back, on a band of whalebone to hold it firm. When she moves, it sways in time with her steps, dips as if nodding. The green in the feathers picks out the green in her eyes and makes them glow. She is fantastical, exotic, bizarre, unique, bewitching. She regards herself in the mirror, almost grudging in her approval.

"It's perfect, Cerridwen. Utterly perfect. Thank you." She sweeps out of the room, down to join the sounds of the ball, swathed in her outrageous dress that will briefly stop all movement, talk, and time when she appears. She will create a scandal. Her uncle will burn with desire, jealousy, but he must not reveal himself. It's bad enough the servants whisper about him; it would not do for people of his own class to know the truth.

He does, however, take his niece's arm for the first dance, holding her close, mesmerized by the feathered eyes of her dress that seem to watch him constantly.

Finn, sitting at one of the library windows, a book open but unattended to in his lap, watches Aurora through the thick glass. At her insistence, three targets are lined up behind the house, in a space too small, really, for archery practice. She has been besting three of her suitors for the past hour and they still seem to find it charming—she is beautiful and rich, after all, and a man can briefly forgive many things when these two virtues are so in evidence.

A hard hand clamps down on Finn's shoulder. He starts, the book falls from his lap and onto the foot of Master Justin, who does not let the boy go. He glares, his mouth set in a hard line, Finn's in a trembling one. In the ghostly mirror of the window, they look rather alike.

"You. You belong to that little Welsh bitch?" Justin spits, turning the boy this way and that, examining him like something to be held up to the light.

"Cerridwen is my mother. She is Welsh," says the boy obliquely, wishing himself big enough to hurt this man.

"How old are you?"

"Seven."

Justin lets him go, dropping him as a dog does a bone it suddenly finds boring. "Stay out of my library."

Finn scrambles to the door, opens it, is stopped by Justin's next question. "What is your name?"

Finn does not answer, knowing there is power in names, and escapes down the corridor as fast as he can. Justin doesn't follow. He stands at the window, watching his niece torment her beaux.

"Butterfly wings," says Aurora. "A dress of butterfly wings, Cerridwen?"

Cerridwen nods slowly, formulates one of her rare sentences. "I will need a net."

"The housekeeper is to give you whatever you need." Aurora smiles at Finn as he huddles on the bed, not calmly sitting on the edge this time, but curled against the wall, as if this is safest. "Did he scare you much?"

Finn shakes his head, wonders how she knows.

"You look like us, that's all," she says. "It scares *him*." She turns again to Cerridwen. "Doesn't he, Cerridwen? Doesn't he look like a De Freitas?"

Cerridwen chooses not to answer, opens her box of threads to select the bobbin of her finest silk. She pulls at the loose end, reels it out a little and holds it up, examining the miniscule thread. Aurora contemplates the pale fluff of hair for a moment, then, flicking Finn a strange smile, she mouths *little cousin* and leaves.

In his short life, Finn has occasionally speculated about his father's identity, about how Cerridwen came to have a child so young. He doesn't ask her, so she never tells.

Finn marvels at his mother; he cannot even begin to think how she gathered so many butterflies and persuaded them to give up their wings, let alone how she coaxed them all into the dress that now drapes Aurora's tall form. It hangs like silk, an empire waist this time, and a foot-long train that seems not to touch the floor, but float above it, carried by still-fluttering wings.

Aurora's black hair has been piled onto her head, then teased out on either side. Jeweled butterflies from London's finest jeweler nestle there, catching the light and throwing it back out.

"Thank you, Cerridwen. Once again, it's perfect. Goodnight. Goodnight, Finn."

Finn awakes to the sound of a struggle. A figure leans over Cerridwen's bed and he can make out in the moonlight his tiny mother, fighting fiercely.

"Give it up. Give it up, little whore, you didn't fight this much last time!" The voice is lustful, frustrated.

Finn throws himself at the shadow-man. Justin curses and kicks him aside, but Finn surges forward once again, fiercely determined, ignoring the pain of Justin's blows.

Justin gives up, shakes the boy off and backs away from the bed, re-buttoning his trousers. He points at Cerridwen, bathed in moonlight and so pale she might be a ghost. "I can take him away any time. Remember that! Any time!"

He slams the door behind him and Finn climbs into his mother's bed. She holds him tightly, rocking; neither of them falls asleep.

Aurora asks for her final dress, a dress made only of words. Cerridwen shakes, balks, refuses to meet the girl's eyes. Aurora drops to her knees beside the seamstress. She takes the tiny, needle-scarred hand and whispers, "They say the Welsh witches are the most dangerous, because it's so hard to tell who they are."

She stands. "A dress of words, Cerridwen. Everything hangs on this, for both of us. You know the words but I shall write them down for you, so you do not forget."

In the deepest part of the Common, far away from the house in Russell Square, Cerridwen sits on the night-damp ground with a piece of parchment beside her. She has collected thistles, spider webs, and a bottle filled with moonlight from a night long ago. She piles the three ingredients onto a small pyre of twigs and kindling, and lights them with a tinderbox. She begins to sing, her voice light, beautiful, fine as the spider webs, bright as the moonlight, and sharp as the thistles. She knows the words by heart, barely looks at the piece of parchment as she sings, conjuring the dress from air and moonlight and words. It forms like a ghost, coalescing above the tiny fire, eddying in the evening breeze.

Finn, having crept out of the house to follow her, watches from behind a tree trunk as she takes a thin knife from her pocket, draws it across her palm and sprinkles blood over the already-dying fire. The dress solidifies, hangs in the air over the smouldering coals as if caught on an invisible hook. It shimmers like gossamer and, if he concentrates, Finn thinks he can see words flying around inside it, whirling like stars being born and dying, creating a universe all within the warp and weft of the dress.

Cerridwen seems smaller; this has cost her much.

The newspaper reports of what happened that night vary, but they agree that Master Justin De Freitas died horribly.

His niece entered the ballroom, all eyes upon her. She wore a strange gown, grey and shimmering, a fabric seemingly alive, but it was hard to tell; the dress defied the eye. Many of the guests had simply wanted to see what she would wear next; tales of her dresses had echoed throughout Society, and they found this one strangely disappointing. All most witnesses could say was that it was grey.

Aurora stood at the top of the great curved staircase, smiling down at the assembly. Master Justin waited at the bottom of the stairs, staring up at his niece in a manner some described as "adoring", others as "inappropriate". She began to descend and by the time she was mid-way down the staircase, those nearest him noticed smoke coming from Master Justin's jacket. At first it seemed to be steam but then the odour of smoke (of sulphur, some said) began to tickle noses. It took Master Justin himself some time to notice, but when the first flames licked from the tongues of his shoes, then up his trousers, shirt, and frock coat and finally reached his cravat, it most certainly had his attention.

His screams were awful, as was the smell, overpoweringly brimstone, and, some said, something even less savoury: the scent of spilled seed.

The immolation happened all too quickly, there was nothing anyone could do. The guests departed rapidly, so there was no one to see the tiny Welsh seamstress and her fragile son creep down the stairs behind Aurora and peer at the smouldering heap of charred humanity and once-fine green velvet frock coat.

"Was he my father?" I asked, but Cerridwen did not answer— she no longer had words. She used them all in the making of Aurora's dress.

That night, Aurora spirited us away, to the grey stone house in Kent. The same Aurora who came to us ten years later, tired of her travels and eager for a quiet place to rest. Cerridwen, worn out by her spell and spending her final years on endless fancywork and embroidery, succumbed and died soon after. The same Aurora who, although my cousin by some counts, stayed with me and lived as my wife these past seventy years.

The very same Aurora De Freitas who died six months ago and left me alone in the grey stone house with only my memories, a peacock feather, butterfly wings and a scrap of parchment.

THE GIRL WITH NO HANDS

THE GIRL WITH NO HANDS

The Devil reclines on the rails of the old bridge, picking at his teeth with a long fingernail.

He's well dressed, handsome, looks like a feckless youth with nothing better to do. In many ways, it's the truth. A fallen angel, a disinherited son, he must pass his days as well as he can, taking not-so-subtle revenge on his father. Today, though, things are a little different.

The Devil has it in mind to take a bride. Not just any bride, but one as pure as she is beautiful, kind, gentle and pious. He could have his choice of glorious succubi, but what he wants is the thing he cannot have. He has chosen his playing field, set his pieces, and is waiting on the bridge for the pawn to arrive. He does not have to wait long.

The man is short, stout, balding. He is bowed under the weight of a sack, and leaves a thin golden trail behind him as wheat pours pitifully from a torn corner. The Devil smiles as the man looks up. The old man nods as well as he can to the handsome youth and continues on.

"Stay a while, good man, I'm in the mood for a chat," begins the Devil.

Reluctantly, the man drops his sack and leans against the bridge for support. "What would you like to discuss, young sir?"

"What would you like best in life?" The Devil is charming when he chooses, for it's easier for him to get his own way.

"I'd like to not be carrying sacks about the place." He wipes the sweat from his face. "I'd like to be rich, that's for sure—rich and able to employ a boy to do my carting for me."

"Then so it shall be if you agree to a trade." Lucifer smiles winningly. "Let me have whatever is sitting in your backyard when you return home."

The Miller thinks of the apple tree and its reaching limbs, of the discarded barrels lying in the grass, of the fat gray mouser stalking its prey, and he laughs. "Surely, young man, you shall have your way. It's a deal."

He knows the lad is either touched or having a joke at his expense. The sack is not so heavy when he picks it up, as if the joke has lightened all his burdens.

"Excellent, good fellow! I shall call by tomorrow morning to collect my prize." He leans back on the struts, well pleased, and watches the Miller, who is convinced he will never see the youth again, stagger away beneath his load.

Miller is still chuckling when he rounds the corner of his house. His heart contracts to something small and cold. Beneath the arms of the apple tree his daughter, her hair glinting in the sun, breaks into an impromptu jig. She smiles: Jephtha's daughter dancing for her father's return.

The girl watches herself in the mirror.

Her hair is platinum and her eyes silver as the moon, in a face with the slightest blush of pink in her cheeks. On her wrists are two bracelets, plaited bands of gold and silver that appeared there not half an hour before her father returned home. These are her bride-gifts; they have grown on her like something organic but malevolent.

Madchen slips the straps of her shift from her shoulders. It pools at her feet as her eyes move across what will soon belong to someone else. Pouting breasts, firm curving hips, pink lips at the apex of her long thighs. She is a prize by any standard.

Her parents have been yelling for almost an hour. Hilde, fearful of the chests that now overflow with treasure, demands to know what her husband has done. When he told his story, she shrieked and beat him about the head. He defended himself as well as he could until she said, *Do you not know who that was?* A name slipped from her lips in a whisper and took the fight from him. He dropped his hands to let her do her worst. Madchen went to her room.

The Devil watches her from the other side of the mirror. He traces her shape with his sharp nails, an artist etching her into mercury, a silver princess to be caught forever. The planes of her face, the curves of her body, the hints of her secret places, all are recorded by his tracing talon. His tongue protrudes as he performs his art in anticipation of the taste of her flesh. He leans forward ...

Madchen, sensing someone watching, throws a shawl over the mirror, tucking it tightly around so that whatever watches her cannot climb out.

No matter to the Devil, he will have her soon enough.

Madchen stands beneath the apple tree, in the center of a chalk circle. Every inch of her skin has been scrubbed until it glows pink.

Hilde, desperate in her maternal rage, had scoured her memory for knowledge to protect her only child. All she could come up with was the chalk circle and the cleaner-than-clean skin. She knows her daughter's heart is pure and there is no more she can do to protect the girl. She prays it will be enough.

The Devil ambles into the yard at the appointed time. He could appear in a flash of fire but does not want to seem ostentatious to his bride. As he approaches, however, Lucifer, the shining one, finds that she hurts his eyes. He stalks toward her and stops short of the chalk circle. He hisses at Madchen; she draws back—his breath smells like brimstone.

"Come out of that circle at once!"

"I will not, sir."

"Come out! I demand it!"

"Again, sir, I will not. No bride for you today," Madchen sings sweetly. Hilde watches her daughter.

"Stay right there, my dove. He cannot harm you."

Lucifer swings around. He sees a mother's love, a mother's will, and smoke rises from his skin. Hilde wishes that she had thought of a circle for herself and her foolish husband.

"She will be mine, woman." Lucifer turns his gaze on the Miller. "Give her no water with which to wash. I will claim her when she is dirty."

"But, sir ..."

"And as for you, interfering woman." The Devil points a long finger at Hilde. She gasps and falls, lying horribly still in the dirt.

Madchen moves to leave the circle.

"No! Stay there, daughter. I will see to your mother," sobs Miller as he lifts Hilde's dead weight. "Your mother would want you safe."

The Devil smiles and disappears.

The night passes with thoughts, and wonders, and dust storms.

Madchen wonders that her mother had to die when her father caused all the trouble. The dust storms pound her with dirt, and filth clings to her skin as tightly as the bracelets on her wrists. When dawn raises her head, Miller comes out, and Lucifer appears, this time in full flame.

"My mother?" Madchen asks.

Miller sobs. "Gone. Hilde is gone."

The Devil approaches in a leisurely fashion. He notes the smut adhering to his bride and smiles. Madchen begins to cry. She weeps so much that the tears wash the dirt from her hands. Lucifer screams his frustration.

"Miller! In the house!"

Miller follows the fallen angel. Madchen knows without a doubt that she cannot bear to lose both parents, not even her fatally flawed father.

The Devil stalks into the tiny parlor where Hilde lies quiet and cold. He does not give her a second glance. Miller stands in the heat of Lucifer's gaze, head bowed, fearing his own death more than the loss of his child.

"Miller, you will cut her hands off. I cannot take her while any part of her is clean."

"No! I will not harm my child further."

"You will or I will take you in her place," says the Devil quite reasonably.

"I cannot ..."

"Father, you must." Madchen has left the chalk circle; her gleaming hands hurt Lucifer's eyes. He cannot look directly at her, she is too terrible, too clean, too pure. He wants her punished, maimed for slighting a prince of heaven. "Father, do as he says. I cannot bear to lose you, too."

There is much weeping and protesting but at last Miller gives in to the combined urgings of his daughter and the Devil. Beneath the apple tree, Madchen places her shining arms on the chopping block, urging her father to strike just above her bridal bracelets, just above the gleaming flesh.

His axe is sharp and he hits the mark once, twice! Madchen screams and the Devil laughs for glee. The girl begins to cry again and her tears wash the bloody stumps until they cease to bleed. Miraculously they heal and the Devil curses, knowing himself defeated once more.

"Sacrifice! Stinking self-sacrifice, you bitch!" He screams and throws a bolt of lightning that splits the apple tree in two. Leaning in to Madchen's face, he whispers with all his venom. "I cannot take you now and you think you've escaped me, little maiden, little Madchen, but know this: I will dog your steps. I will put chasms beneath your feet. I will raise mountains in your path. You could have ruled at my side, but you chose *this*."

He disappears in a puff of smoke, leaving his unwilling bride and her father to clear up the remains of her limbs.

"Stay with me, Madchen," sobs Miller. "I can look after you—"

"With the Devil's wealth, Father?" She shakes her head and clumsily pushes open the door with her stumps. "I will not stay here. It will be too easy for him to find me. And I cannot stay with you, knowing that you've caused my mother's death and my maiming."

Miller weeps. "I beg you ..."

"A waste of time, a waste of breath. I will go into the world. Strangers cannot treat me any worse than my own father has."

Madchen takes neither food nor drink. Random kindness, she thinks, will be her only hope. Her life is not under her control; she has learned this harshly, but having learned the lesson, she will live by it.

Lucifer watches her progress. His room is limitless, all the mirrors in the world back onto it like windows to the world above. He calls this space his crucible, where he ferments all ill—for the Devil lives behind mirrors. In the centre of the room is a great pool of molten fire in which he watches the world at large—the mirrors he uses to peer into lives and hearts, but the pool is his main informant.

He becomes bored with the repetition of her days. She walks, she starves. She grows thinner, the flesh melting back until she is bone with a canvas of skin stretched across her frame. She is still beautiful, shining like a saint in the grip of martyrdom. It makes him angrier and angrier but he cannot put his mind to revenge quite yet for he simply does not know what to *do* to her. After all, he has taken her mother, her hands, her father, all of her illusions. As far as the Devil can see, she is as low as she can get without death.

When and if she rises again (and he has no real doubt that she will for there is something about this girl that says *indomitable*), he will raise his hand against her once more.

For the moment he leaves his mirrors and turns his attention elsewhere. Perhaps for a few months, perhaps for years—time moves differently for him. He turns away, catching sight of the silvered portrait he made of her not many days since; his eyes rake the surface until the mercury bubbles and slides from the back of the mirror. The silvered princess is no more, her place in eternity gone.

A pear tree, illuminated by the full moon, catches her eye. She has been two weeks without food and it seems as though her belly has crept back to stick to her spine. The pears are perfect, just on the turn from green to gold, and she knows they will be firm to the bite, then yielding and sweet, white flesh filled with juice. Her stomach growls loudly in the darkness.

Madchen starts forward; surely there will be some pears on the ground fit for eating. After a few steps, her feet sink and she stumbles back. A moat surrounds the orchard, wide and deep and impassable for a girl with no hands. She cannot swim.

She sits heavily at the edge of the moat, her feet in the water, her head resting on her stumps, and weeps for the first time since leaving home. Her tears are fat; despair makes them heavy as they fall into the water.

Madchen looks across at the impossible orchard. The water swirls around her ankles, shifts and heaves into the shape of a woman. The undine regards her curiously.

"You have given of yourself. What will you have in return?"

Madchen is too surprised to speak and the undine becomes impatient. "You have given your tears. You must ask something in return."

"Those pears," says Madchen. "I must eat and I've a notion for those pears."

"Those pears are counted," says the sprite obliquely. Nevertheless, she bows her head and the waters part until Madchen can walk across the damp floor of the moat and struggle up the bank. She turns to offer thanks but the undine has melted back into her element, and the moat is whole once more.

The pears grow beyond her reach. She leans her head against the trunk of the nearest tree. The dryad who lives within feels the splash of tears against the bark, and her boughs creak. Madchen steps back hastily to find the branches have lowered, and fat, juicy pears are at the perfect height. She stretches her swan's neck and bites into the flesh of the nearest fruit. She eats until her poor, abused belly protests at this gluttony so soon on the tail of starvation.

The morning mist melts as the king takes his daily walk in the orchard. He has slipped the eyes of the court and made his way to the clump of reeds where the head gardener hides a small rowboat. The king enjoys this little piece of freedom, the blisters the oars make on his hands, the satisfying splash of the water as he rows across to his orchard with its counted pears.

He makes his way through the trees, idly numbering the fruits as he passes. His Majesty likes the pear trees, he thinks them elegant with their silvered leaves and green-gold fruit. When he reaches the final tree he frowns and re-counts the pears. Their number has dwindled since yesterday. He will have the culprit found, he vows, and then he sees her.

She still sleeps, her long body stretched in exhaustion, breathing with the rhythm of a wave. She is silvery like his pear trees, gleaming like a moonbeam. He kneels beside her, his head tilted, and surveys her face, the slow rise and fall of her breasts, and the strangely smooth stumps at the ends of her beautifully-formed arms. She is ever-so-slightly pear-shaped and this pleases him.

He settles beside her to wait. He has plenty of time. She will be his wife, this little pear-thief. His sensibilities are highly tuned to beauty, to refinement, to grace, and this girl pleases him on all counts. In his way, he's like Lucifer: sure of himself and certain that no one will gainsay his wishes.

He will have hands made for her, limbs crafted by his most cunning smiths, silver to match her hair and her sheen. His silver bride. He imagines the coolness of their touch on his skin, of their unyielding firmness, of the ridges made by decorative engravings. He imagines her mouth making up for the shortcomings of her other limbs. He smiles, well-pleased.

The Queen settles her silver hands on her swollen belly as if she can feel the life stirring inside her.

The Queen Mother, Constance, watches this movement and her heart flips painfully, as it is wont to do when her daughter-in-law's handicap pierces her. Pity, sadness, pain, and love all wash over her. Most of all there is love, for the Queen Mother has come to care for Madchen more than she does for her son. It's something to do with the girl's helplessness. Sons grow up and no longer *need* their mothers but daughters always do. Or they always *want* to need their mothers, perhaps that's why the bond seldom breaks.

Madchen's mother, as Constance knows, is gone, murdered most foully. And the girl, maimed by her own father, is still *good*.

This amazes Constance most of all, the girl's inherent goodness. She is kind, generous to a fault, gentle, graceful, as lovely as the moon, a misplaced gem of a Miller's daughter. Constance can see why the Devil himself wanted her—for all the perversity of his desire, she is a supremely perfect wife.

Her silver hands rub her belly. Constance knows she can feel nothing, that she will never be able to feel the warmth of her child beneath her fingertips, nor will she be able to defend that child or herself against harm, for although the silver limbs are beautiful and convincing, they have no purpose beyond a cosmetic one. They have no movement, no malleability, no facility or functionality.

Constance moves closer to Madchen. She does not touch her for that would be inappropriate in public, but hopes her sympathy will be obvious to her daughter-in-law. They stand on the steps of the palace waiting for the king.

Beyond the walls his armies are massed: today he goes to war. He has charged his mother with Madchen's care, and that of his unborn. He does not envisage the battle will last more than a few years.

The king strides down the stairs and bows farewell to his mother. He holds Madchen tenderly, running his hands over her metallic limbs so he will remember their feel, then up to the fleshy parts of her arms more briefly. Her mouth he tastes as if he already misses it and its skills. Finally, he places one of his gauntleted hands on her belly, where his son turns and kicks in response. The king smiles and finishes his journey to the courtyard, where a warhorse awaits.

Madchen watches him leave. She cannot imagine her hours and days without this man she has grown to love so. The years before him seem unreal and, now, strange. The place where she stores her grief begins to ache as this loss of her husband makes room for itself there.

Her face, notes the Devil, has not changed. Luminous, a little fuller, her eyes the same shimmering grey he remembers. She is now a definite pear-shape, with her little bundle of the king's joy wiggling inside her.

He drags a thoughtful nail across his cheek, pondering how best to start.

"Was his father so handsome?" Madchen's laughter is limned with hysteria. It is only a few hours since the child pushed his way into the world after a long labor. Her son's eyes are slitted with newborn's ecstasy at finding a full breast. He hiccups and his mother wipes the thin dribble of milk from his tiny lips. Soon full, his head slips, lips surrendering their determined hold on her nipple as he begins to snore softly, almost a kitten's purr. The weight of the child, his smell, seem to dampen the pain Madchen feels at her husband's absence. Or perhaps it just makes it easier to ignore the ache. Constance smiles down at them.

"Never so handsome. He looked like a shaved little monkey, all red wrinkles. And yelling! Born yelling." She runs a gentle finger down her grandson's downy cheek; when he stirs in his sleep she pulls back. "What will you call him? We must have a name to tell his father."

"Hildebrand." Madchen speaks quickly as if this thought has been hovering at her lips for some time, waiting to be spoken. "For my mother's memory."

Briefly, Constance is bitten by jealousy but it flies as soon as Madchen's cold hand touches her arm and the girl smiles with the warmth of a hearth-fire, seeking approval.

"It is good. A strong name, Madchen. I will write this to your husband." She kisses the girl's brow and brushes a hand across Hildebrand's face. "Rest now, my girl. I will visit you this evening."

As the Queen Mother departs, waves of ladies-in-waiting cluster about Madchen's bed to fuss over her and the heir.

"My Dearest Boy, Madchen has given you a son and your kingdom an heir. She has named him Hildebrand, a fine name. Both are doing well, my son. I pray you will return to us soon. God's speed. Your Loving Mother, Constance."

Lucifer finishes reading the letter aloud, his voice falsetto and bitter. The messenger who carries it is asleep under a tree, filled with ale generously provided by the fine young gentleman he met on the road.

The Devil pushes a thoughtful breath from his lips and lifts his hand. As his fingers pass over the parchment the letters dance and jumble, like feet on hot coals. He reads it aloud once more, his voice his own, his smile fat and happy.

The king slumps in the saddle. A letter arrived this morning. Before his unseeing eyes, his army sprawls like a field of poppies in their red armor.

My Dearest Son, your wife has given birth to a monster, a child with the head of a dog. She is cursed. Pray tell me how to deal with this abomination. Your Loving Mother, Constance.

A soldier approaches, the naked blade of his sword catching the sunlight, and the king is reminded of his wife's sheen. He rouses himself, startled. Madchen has been nothing but a loving wife. She has never shown a sign of being anything other than she appears: a sweet, gentle, kind girl. If they have been afflicted with this burden, then they shall bear it together.

"Where is my scribe? I would have him take a letter."

"Now, your Majesty?"

"Now."

Royal messengers really aren't what they used to be, thinks the Devil as the man's snoring rings in his ears. He turns his attention to the letter, which astounds him.

This man, this idiot king, still wants his wife. Loves her, supports her, bids her have courage in the face of her adversity; bids her be strong until he returns and they will shoulder their burden together. What does he think? That they will teach their dog-headed son to fetch?

He spits his disgust and the letters dance once more. There will be no more joy for Madchen.

Constance lifts her head and wipes her mouth, thankful that no one is around to see her illness. Her son's letter sent her for the basin on first reading and the sensation did not lessen with the second. She has put it aside, determined not to read it again.

From the window she can see Madchen and Hildebrand. The boy is almost a year old now but the size of a child twice that age, straight and stocky as his father was. He is a determined, curious child, fearless. He loves his mother with all his heart.

Madchen speaks with the head gardener as the boy plays with the palace wolfhounds. The beasts tower over him but they are tender, never too rough. Madchen, ever an attentive mother, raises her eyes regularly to check on him as she discusses her plans for a new garden.

Constance looks over her shoulder to the letter. It moves, caught by a breeze, as animated as the malice it contains.

Kill them both. Destroy the corruption. Cut out their tongues and eyes to prove you have obeyed your king. Do not hesitate, Mother, strike swiftly.

The Queen Mother gingerly folds the letter and slides it to the bottom of a jewellery box. Her hands tremble as she contemplates her next step. She will do her duty as a mother and as a regent.

"Hello, little queen."

Madchen, drenched by his voice, turns to face him squarely. She feels her son wiggling on her back and wills him not to draw attention to himself.

"What's that, my sweet? Offspring?" He swings down from the branch. He has been waiting for two days while she trudged away from the palace. "What lovely silver hands you have."

Still, she does not speak.

"Still alive, I see. *Tsk tsk*. Naughty Constance disobeying her son's orders. It's a sad state of affairs when you can't trust the Queen Mother."

"Why? Why do you dog my steps? You could have anyone you wanted; why me?" She despairs. "Why won't you leave me alone?"

"Because you said *no*." He leans in close, his long nails playing across her face as gently as a breeze. "But you can change it all, you know. You still fascinate me, damn you. Say *yes*, now."

Madchen stands on tiptoe and kisses him. He will, he thinks, be merciful, now that she has been brought low, and she still makes him ache: his love and hate entwine like mating snakes. She pulls back, fixes him with her argent eyes and gives him a hard smile.

"You will never know the taste of me again. I hope the memory of that kiss lingers until the last trumpet sounds."

He strikes out and she falls but does not hit the ground even though her child and clothes do. Thousands of feathers break through the parchment of her skin. Her silver hands, immune to eldritch change, clatter on the stones of the path as, instinctively, she beats the air with new wings.

Hildebrand stops crying and stares at the large, snowy white owl. Madchen lets out a screech of anguish.

"Enjoy your life, Madchen. Try looking after your child with nothing but feathers." He will think, from time to time, of the feathered maiden but he will not imagine she might escape his malice.

He disappears before she can finish her swoop at his head and her claws meet nothing but air. She settles beside Hildebrand, a picture of despair, and her son's hand reaches out to stroke her. He presses his face to her feathers and notes, to his comfort, that she still smells like his mother.

Time and guilt have bent Constance like metal subjected to a fierce heat.

It is four years since she sent her daughter-in-law and grandson into the woods. The eyes and tongue of a gentle hind and her fawn float in a sealed glass jar, awaiting her son's request for proof. She received no acknowledgement of her last letter. Indeed, no word has come from her son at all, although troubadours and tinkers bring news of how he continues his war.

Letters bring her nothing but dread and the one that arrived today lies on a bureau, set aside from the documents she is signing. Her secretary pours hot, red wax onto the documents then stamps the royal seal into the molten mess as it cools. When the pile of papers has disappeared she turns her attention to the letter. The parchment crackles under her hands as she breaks the seal.

Her son returns, within the week, his war won, his dominions safe.

Constance folds the letter and adds it to the small archive in the jewellery box where her son's inhuman instructions have lived these last years. She slips away, down the staircase leading to her private garden.

In a pear tree sits the large white owl that has taken to visiting her. The creature is truly beautiful, an artwork with strange silver eyes. Constance scratches at the bird's neck and it emits a soft, sad sound.

"I'm so scared, my lovely owl. My son returns and I will see once and for all if he is a monster. What if this man who came from me is something less than I believed him to be?" She sighs. "Tell me, white owl, will it hurt more or less?"

The creature starts and screeches. Her wings stretch wide and she takes off as if startled by the news. Constance watches her go, bereft.

The owl circles down into a clearing. Dryads have coaxed their trees to weave branches into a roof, climbing vines and shrubs form the walls of a small hut. It is simple but comfortable, made with care.

In the clearing stands a boy, big for his age. A quiver of handmade arrows is slung across his back and a bow is in his hand. He sets snares and hunts for food now that he is old enough; but he never hunts the birds of the air. The storm of his mother's wings draws his attention and he watches her graceful landing, marvelling as always.

He is a child of silence: he has no memory of human speech, nor can he speak the language of birds. Communication between mother and son is rudimentary, one of love, not of sound. Hildebrand does not feel the loss, but it frustrates Madchen, for she had words before this time of feathers.

How can she tell her son that his father returns? How can she tell him that they are in danger? She will defend her child to the death. She does not know if it will be enough.

The king wanders.

Constance showed him the jar containing evidence of his wife and son's fate. He struck her, would have drawn his sword had she not pulled the letters from the jewellery box and thrown them at him. Their contents stayed his hand and broke his heart. Finally, Constance, assured of his innocence in the matter, told him of their exile. He vowed to find them and set off through the private garden, into the woods, with neither food nor drink nor companions to sustain him.

That was five days ago and his kingly garb is ragged and dirty; he looks like a beggar. His boots, right enough for riding, are not meant for walking miles and miles across forest floors. He discarded them on the second day, finding the blisters too painful to continue shod. Forest creatures play in and around the stinking leather as the king stumbles deeper into the woods.

He finds a stream and follows it, lapping at the crystal water from time to time in the hope that it will stop his belly from constant complaint. Any extra flesh he may once have carried has disappeared and his mind is strangely clear, freed of earthly considerations. If he cannot find his wife, his love, his beloved burden, there is nothing in life for him.

Then there is his son. The child is not real to him; Hildebrand is merely a concept, a chimera. The king has no memory of touch, or sound, or smell on which to hang his heart. His child is a lesson he must learn. If he can find him.

A clearing opens before him. Woven branches and vines form a small shelter, outside of which stands a boy. The child sees the man, sees his face stripped clean by suffering, but makes no sound. Behind him, the trees and foliage move and shift, fold back into themselves until the little hut is no more. The child casts a look over his shoulder; his home is gone.

The king takes in the boy, his black hair and sturdy limbs, and starts across the clearing. There is a rush of air, the beating of great wings, and Madchen swoops at him, her talons drawn. He falls, bloody scratches on his face, and the bird plummets to follow up her attack.

The owl's screech is replaced by the screaming of a human voice, long silenced. Hands and fingernails slap and claw at him as he sees his wife's face, transfigured by grief and anger and fear. He does not fight her, merely lies beneath her and watches as her rage plays itself out.

She hears, as her screams subside, his first words to her in almost five years.

"Madchen, my love, my silver bride."

Her hands fail her, her rage washes away like an ebb tide. She sobs and collapses. Her husband wraps his arms around her and holds her until she lifts her silvered eyes to his dark ones, to feast upon his face, to consume the changes the years have wrought.

As they kneel in front of each other, Hildebrand approaches, uncertain how to treat this man who may be an enemy, or a friend—he cannot read his mother's strange behaviour. He stands just out of reach.

Madchen raises one hand to her son, keeping the other firmly caught between her husband's palms. Hildebrand stares for a moment then reaches out to touch the white-skinned limb. Madchen's hands, restored to her as wings during her feathered phase, are whole.

The Devil has watched, drawn to a casual mirror visit, his miscalculation causing his jaw to drop. That she would once again be willing to blindly sacrifice herself for someone she loved and so earn release from his spite, did not occur to him—that a fully-limbed owl might become a fully-limbed maiden. He clenches his hands into fists, his nails cutting into the soft flesh (which heals immediately). Lightning spits from his fingertips, he points towards Madchen's image but finds that the silvery sparks go the wrong way, licking up to his wrists, boiling around his own hands. This malignancy will not leave *him*. His shoulders slump, defeated.

Husband and son each hold one of the pale hands in wonder as they rise, the little family, and begin their journey to the castle where Constance waits with watchful eyes and an anxious heart.

AFTERWORD

If ever there was a question which has the power to induce a stroke on a writer, (or at the very least a fit of apoplexy), it's: "Where do you get your ideas from?" On good days, I wave my hands vaguely and shrug. On the less-good days, I insist that they all come from www.awesomeideas.com.

Admittedly, neither of these answers helps anyone. The spark of an idea can come from something as mundane as looking at the shapes in the coffee grounds at the bottom of a cup, or a supernova collision of thoughts at just the right time—and in the right place. Hopefully, you have a pen and paper handy, because shower-ideas (those which occur in the shower) are the worst—scribbling a brilliant plot outline on a steamy mirror just doesn't cut it. Trust me.

So I thought I might disclose the genesis of each of the stories, as well as I can remember them. Or lie about them. Y'know, whatever.

Bluebeard

This is a version of the old tale and was one of the stories I wrote for my Masters. The first line popped into my head and I knew it was a young girl watching her mother, loving her but judging her. The setting of the French bordello and then the country house were both very clear, and I liked the concept of walls being both a protection and a prison. My heroine is a mix of both immense intellect and a childish need for a mother's love and protection—and she's desperate to know she'll always come first in her mother's heart. Even though—or perhaps particularly because—this was a version of Bluebeard, I wanted my female characters to survive, for mother and daughter to save each other. I also liked the idea that the slaughterer in this case was a woman; a crone, quite fearsome and judgmental, threatened and vicious about sexuality and its open display. This story first appeared in *Shimmer* #4 (Summer 2006 issue), and it gained an Honourable Mention in the 2007 *Year's Best Fantasy and Horror* (ed. Ellen Datlow, Kelly Link and Gavin Grant).

The Living Book

At first I was thinking about a woman whose body was made up of the leaves of a book that could be peeled back so you could read her. Further contemplation changed it to her having the ability to make the text appear on her body as and when requested—the words of any book. I liked the idea of her being one of the treasures of Byzantium: I imagined this adorned woman moving slowly and elegantly through the ornate and formal corridors of a palace, and then riding in a chariot like a Roman triumph. Although she was a created thing she had developed a personality—the wants and desires and needs of any human. When those needs were not met or recognised—particularly the needs for love and care—her reaction was perhaps both less than and at the same time *extraordinarily* human. This story has not been previously published.

The Jacaranda Wife

I'd had the idea of jacaranda women in my head for a while. My study looks out into the backyard where there is a giant jacaranda tree and one rainy day I was writing—or rather, not so much writing as staring out the window at the tree, which was in season and the bunches of purple flowers were so heavy with rain that they looked, well, pregnant—so that's where that idea came from originally. I hadn't written any stories set specifically in Australia, so I thought it was something I would/should try, to set a tale against a very Australian landscape. My mother's family came to Australia with the Second Fleet and settled in Port Macquarie initially, and their family property was called Rollands Plain. The idea of the woman going back into the tree came from having an Irish character and the Irish legends of selkie wives whose skins are stolen by their husbands. The jacaranda has been transplanted all over the world—just like ideas and stories and fairytales—and I like the sense of it not quite belonging, of a strangeness in the landscape. This story is an Australian fable, which has roots in a European fairytale tradition. This story was first published in Jack Dann's *Dreaming Again* in 2008 and gained an Honourable Mention in the 2008 *Year's Best Horror* edited by Ellen Datlow (2009).

Red Skein

This a reworking of Little Red Riding Hood, inspired by Angela Carter's *The Company of Wolves*, and it is another of the stories from my Masters. I liked the idea of Little Red being not only brave but far more dangerous than she was depicted in the later versions of the fairytale. I was also exploring the idea of the frictions between parents and children, specifically how mothers often want to see themselves in their daughters. When they instead see a difference, often a terrible unrecognisable difference—they can react badly. This story first appeared in *Walking Bones Magazine*, Fall 2006 issue.

The Chrysanthemum Bride

In 2006 I read about two men in a remote part of China who had been murdering prostitutes and selling them as brides for afterlife marriage to families who'd lost unmarried sons. The idea was so weird and so grotesque and so strangely juxtaposed in modern society that it stuck in my bowerbird brain. I couldn't get the story to shift onto the page, though, until a few months later when I was on a visit to Sydney and went to an art gallery and saw the quote that appears at the beginning of the story. Everything fell into place—I could see the main character and the setting and everything. I actually scribbled the story during a Billy Crystal performance at the Princess Theatre! This story was first published at *Fantasy Magazine* in December 2009.

Frozen

Believe it or not this was inspired by watching the film *Kinky Boots*. The opening scene has a little boy alone on a boardwalk, with his father (I think) inside drinking. I had been thinking about lost children, how parents can be so careless with their offspring, and how society makes great noise about protecting kids but all of this doesn't seem to stop the flow of discarded children. I also wanted to write a story in which you couldn't really tell if the narrator was a male or female. I know some readers find this frustrating, but it was an experiment in voice for me and I like the result. This story was first published in *Mort Castle's Doorways Magazine*, Issue 8, April 2009.

The Hummingbird Heart

Some years ago I read an Aztec fairytale called *The Hummingbird's Fear*, which posits the idea that hummingbirds were sprung from a woman's guilty heart—which is an awesome concept. The only similarity with this work is that there's a hummingbird involved. I woke up from a dream of a mother putting a metal box into her child's chest; the more I thought about it the more I wondered what you might put into the box to simulate a heartbeat. The natural answer seemed to be an immortal hummingbird—but of course! I liked the idea of transplanting the hummingbird to the Aegean—where they do not naturally occur—because it was also a kind of a transplant and a colonisation of Antiope. This story was first published in the Spring 2008 issue of *Shimmer* and garnered an Honourable Mention in the 2008 *Year's Best Horror* edited by Ellen Datlow (2009).

Words

This story is the result of a mash-up of ideas (so nothing new there). I love Anne Sexton's poem *Words*, and it had me thinking about the power of words—and this idea/concept/notion was percolating in the back brain. I re-read *The Pied Piper* and that was in the mental blender too. I seem to recall a period of despair about my writing and the elements in my head combined to create this little tale. Perhaps I was just trying to make myself feel better. My house and the house next door are very close together, but I swear that's as far as things go. I do not own a green robe. This story was first published in issue #5 of an awesome little Australian journal called *The Lifted Brow* and was shortlisted for the Aurealis Award for Best Fantasy Short Story 2009.

The Little Match Girl

This is the first fairytale I remember my mother reading to me, most probably because it all ended in tears. Andersen's *The Little Match Girl* is so much about first fears: loss, abandonment, being loveless and unloved, needs left unmet, a fate not of one's own choosing. When I rewrote the story, I turned it ever so slightly on its axis: my Little Match Girl remained someone stripped of any helpers or carers, a woman who was abandoned. I wanted my version to give her agency and choice—that she choose her own end. So, I started to think about who she might have been (rather than a defenceless child), and that's how my girl became someone who stands outside of society and refuses to bend to what others think she should do. I like to think her final words are a declaration of independence. This story was first published in *Shimmer* #3, Spring 2006 issue, and gained an Honourable Mention in the 2007 *Year's Best Fantasy and Horror* (ed. Ellen Datlow, Kelly Link and Gavin Grant).

The Juniper Tree

This was also a story written for my Masters. At first I thought I was writing about the victimised child, but the more I read Marina Warner's work in *From the Beast to the Blonde*, the more I realised it was about Second Wife and the plight of second wives in households where their security and economic stability could be threatened by the presence of children from a previous marriage. Historically, security was the key to survival and a woman had to fight to ensure the safety of her own. The idea of a universal female love for all children is entirely misplaced—the family home was the location of a turf war, of which husbands often seemed oblivious. I did, however, like the idea of there being a genuine affection between the step-siblings—who are most often cast in the roles of opponents in traditional fairytales. This story was first published in *Lady Churchill's Rosebud Wristlet* #18, July 2006.

Skin

I wanted a story that reversed the selkie myth and I wanted a tale of revenge and redemption. I'm quite fascinated by the consequences acts of carelessness and anger can have on love, how revenge can be regretted and I really liked the idea of a strangely happy end. This story was first published in *The Lifted Brow* #3, February 2008 issue.

The Bone Mother

I always thought Baba Yaga got a bad rap. I wanted to show her in a different light as someone whose power doesn't lessen as she ages or become malign in her loss of youth and beauty. Here she's a counter-balance to the crone in *Bluebeard*. I wanted my Baba Yaga to be more than a husk; she must be wise, strong, determined, she must stand alone proudly. I also wanted her to be tall and unbowed, for her face to be the map of her life that Vasilissa contemplates. This is the first time this story has been published.

The Dead Ones Dont Hurt You

I wrote this for Clarion South in Trent Jamieson's week. It has been considerably reworked: from a smarmy short it has evolved into something much darker. It sprang out of my vague annoyance with people (generally women) who are so desperate for relationships that they'll put up with anything in order to keep a partner. I then married this initial concept with the tradition of the zombie as a slave (not a Romero-supercharged-brain-eating monster). I wanted to hark back to proper zombie lore, with the creatures as compliant servants who'll return to their graves if fed salt. This is the first time this story has been published.

Light as Mist, Heavy as Hope

This story sprang from one of my stranger ideas. I'd been thinking about how to rework *Rumplestiltzskin* while watching a crime thriller one night, in which a character observed that paedophiles don't wear big signs or the mark of the beast to distinguish them from everyone else. The idea was that it was so damned hard to know who was safe and who wasn't. I'd always wondered about the little fairytale man's motivation—and since Rumplestiltzskin has always creeped me out I just made him a bit creepier. This story was first published in Drollerie Press' anthology *Needles & Bones* in June 2009.

Dresses, Three

This story was commissioned by *Shimmer* for their Art issue in Spring 2008. I was given a piece of art by the amazingly talented Chrissy Ellsworth for inspiration. The piece, "My Life as a Fashion Designer", had a woman with a dress of birds, feathers and words, and I thought about the tale of *Donkeyskin*. The princess in that story demands three dresses of her father, one like the stars, one like the moon, the other like the sun. I knew I wanted one of peacock feathers, one of butterfly wings, but needed to chat with my sister about the form the third dress. Shell helped me get the idea to crystallise. The story was short-listed for the Aurealis Award Best Fantasy Short Story in 2008, and won an Honourable Mention in the 2008 *Year's Best Horror* edited by Ellen Datlow, 2009.

The Girl with No Hands

This story was also written for my Masters and found a home with Gavin and Kelly at *Lady Churchill's Rosebud Wristlet* #23 in 2008. It's a remix of the original German tale with elements of Welsh folklore and other 'bits' from my messy brain thrown in. Again, I wanted to rehabilitate a character who always got a bad rap, the King's mother, and I also wanted the main character Madchen to be a bit more active in what she did instead of just having things happen to her. Plus, I kind of wanted to include a king with a pear fetish.

STORY ACKNOWLEDGEMENTS

"Bluebeard" copyright © Angela Slatter. First published in
    Shimmer #4 (Summer 2006).

"The Living Book" copyright © Angela Slatter. Appears here
    for the very first time.

"The Jacaranda Wife" copyright © Angela Slatter. First
    published in *Dreaming Again*, 2008. Edited by Jack Dann.

"Red Skein" copyright © Angela Slatter. First published in
    Walking Bones Magazine, (Fall 2006).

"The Chrysanthemum Bride" copyright © Angela Slatter. First
    published in *Fantasy Magazine*, (December 2009).

"Frozen" copyright © Angela Slatter. First published in *Mort
    Castle's Doorways Magazine*, Issue 8, (April 2009).

"The Hummingbird Heart" copyright © Angela Slatter. First
    published in *Shimmer* #9 (Spring 2008).

"Words" copyright © Angela Slatter. First published in *The
    Lifted Brow* #5, (June 2009).

"The Little Match Girl" copyright © Angela Slatter. First
    published in *Shimmer* #3 (Spring 2006).

"The Juniper Tree" copyright © Angela Slatter. First published
    in *Lady Churchill's Rosebud Wristlet* #18, (July 2006).

"Skin" copyright © Angela Slatter. First published in *The Lifted
    Brow* #3 (February 2008).

"The Bone Mother" copyright © Angela Slatter. Appears here
    for the very first time.

"The Dead Ones Don't Hurt You" copyright © Angela Slatter.
    Appears here for the very first time.

"Light As Mist, Heavy As Hope" copyright © Angela Slatter.
    First published in *Needles & Bones*, Drollerie Press, 2009.

"Dresses, Three" copyright © Angela Slatter. First published in
    Shimmer #8 (Winter 2008).

"The Girl With No Hands" copyright © Angela Slatter.
    First published in *Lady Churchill's Rosebud Wristlet* #23
    (November 2008).

THANK YOU

The publisher would like to thank Elizabeth Grzyb,
Angela Slatter, Lisa Hannett, Jack Dann, Kim Wilkins,
Simon Brown, Jonathan Strahan, Peter McNamara, Ellen
Datlow, Grant Stone, Jeremy G. Byrne, Sean Williams,
Garth Nix, David Cake, Simon Oxwell, Grant Watson,
Sue Manning, Steven Utley, Bill Congreve, Lisa Bennett,
Terry Dowling, Stephen Dedman, the Mt Lawley Mafia,
the Nedlands Yakuza, Shane Jiraiya Cummings, Angela Challis,
Donna Maree Hanson, Kate Williams, Kathryn Linge, Melissa
Donald, Andrew Williams, Al Chan, Alisa Krasnostein,
everyone I've missed ...

... and *you*.